MERCY

A Neon Lawyer Novel

VICTOR METHOS

Copyright 2016 Victor Methos

Kindle & Print Edition

License Statement

This book is licensed for your personal enjoyment only. This book may not be re-sold or given away to other people. If you would like to share this book with another person, please purchase an additional copy for each recipient. If you're reading this book and did not purchase it, or it was not purchased for your use only, then please return to Amazon.com and purchase your own copy.

Please note that this is a work of fiction. Any similarity to persons, living or dead, is purely coincidental. All events in this work are purely from the imagination of the author and are not intended to signify, represent, or reenact any event in actual fact.

1

Brigham Theodore sat next to his client at the defense table but was so revolted by what he'd done that he couldn't look at him.

The man had an odd body type: no muscle, arms and legs like sticks, just skin and bones… except his belly. Plump and round, it actually protruded onto the table. He'd waxed his mustache, but he kept sticking his fingers in his nose—he'd done it at least twenty times in front of the jury.

The trial had been going for an hour. The officer on the stand, a uniformed rookie who'd been in the Salt Lake Police Department for only four months, was testifying. Brigham tried to concentrate, but he was so nauseated by his client that it was difficult to think about anything else. The image of the poor victim and what he must be going through after an ordeal like this was a pain he didn't want to think about.

The prosecutor was at the lectern, flipping through a few notes before beginning the direct examination of the officer. Marissa Newly, the prosecutor, was a slim woman with raven hair. Several of the male jurors were unable to look anywhere else when she stood up to speak.

"Please state your name for the record," Marissa said.

"Officer Cameron Ray Boyd."

"And where do you work, Officer Boyd?"

"I've been with the Salt Lake PD now for four months."

"And what do you do?"

"I'm a police officer on bike patrol in the downtown area."

Marissa moved a strand of hair behind her ear. "And were you on patrol on the morning of March the second of this year?"

"Yes."

"Do you remember engaging with a member of the public at around nine in the morning?"

"Yes."

"Tell us about it."

The officer cleared his throat. He glanced over at the defense table and then continued. "Um, my partner and I were riding in the area of about 1300 East and Second South when we passed a wooden fence with gaps in it, and holes. Came up about six feet." He cleared his throat again, a slight blush in his cheeks. "As we were passing, I looked through the gaps in the fence and saw what appeared to be a man who was... um, nude."

"Was the man doing anything?"

The officer's brow furrowed and then smoothed. "Yes. I

couldn't make it out at first, so I stopped the bike and peered in through one of the cracks." The officer stopped and took a sip of water from a paper cup on the stand in front of him. "I saw a Caucasian male who was nude from the waist down. He was squatting on his porch and he had a… he had a hat underneath him."

"What kind of hat?"

"Stetson. A cowboy hat."

"What, if anything, was he doing to the hat?"

The officer took another sip of water. "He was defecating into it."

"Define 'defecating' for the jury, please."

The officer's slight blush went to a deep red that ran from just below the eyes to the jaw. "He was pooping into the hat. I don't know how else to put it."

"What did you do?"

"I went around to the gate, and it wasn't locked, so we—"

Someone in the audience shouted, "You son of a bitch! My daddy gave me that hat! You knew it was my favorite."

The judge said, "Sit down, sir. Right now."

The defendant turned around, and Brigham could tell what was about to happen. He moved to stop it, but his client shook him off. The emotions in this case ran too high, and he'd lost control.

"That's what you get," the defendant shouted back. "You

gave me them tools back and the drill didn't work. I shit in your hat now but I'm a shit in your bed next time."

The man in the audience rushed forward, and the defendant was on his feet. Brigham grabbed him, trying to pull him back down, but it was too late. The men collided and rolled over the defense table. They hit the floor, already exchanging blows.

The bailiffs in the courtroom waded in to pull them apart. The judge was yelling and slamming his gavel on its sound block, people in the audience—family members on both sides—were screeching at each other, and one of the bailiffs pulled out a Taser.

"No!" Brigham shouted. "He has a pacemaker!"

The bailiff fired and Brigham tried to pull his client out of the way, but the Taser caught the man in the shoulder and he convulsed so violently that he struck Brigham in the jaw and knocked him down.

Brigham lay on the courtroom floor as people shouted and swore, and the gavel kept pounding. He tried to sit up but decided he'd done all he could do. He'd lie there until the dust settled.

When order had been restored, the defendant and his neighbor had been put in the holding cells of the courthouse. Brigham collapsed into the defense chair, rubbing his jaw. He looked over to Marissa, who had turned a ghostly white. She was new, and this was one of her first trials. He figured she was probably asking herself what she'd gotten into.

"Hey. This is a mistrial, and we're gonna have to do it again. How about no jail and community service with Parks and Rec? You pick the number of hours."

She thought a moment. "Okay," she said. "A hundred hours of community service and one year of probation with a mental health evaluation and counseling. But no service at Parks and Rec. He should do it at the animal shelter to clean up messes like he made."

Brigham nodded. That was probably a good call.

"I'll make him take that." He moved his jaw from side to side. "Can we call the judge back in? My jaw hurts."

2

Brigham sauntered into the Riley Building and stood in the lobby a moment. His jaw, luckily, wasn't broken. The ER had given him an ice pack and ibuprofen and sent him on his way. It seemed like a waste of time, but Brigham had never had health insurance before, and now that he had the money for it, he made certain he used it.

A father and his son waited for the elevator. When the elevator arrived, the father gently pushed the son in. The boy was holding a green balloon and lost his grip on the string. The balloon shot to the ceiling—about twenty feet above them.

"My balloon!"

"We don't have time for that, Spencer."

"Daddy, no!"

Brigham waited and watched the red numbers above the elevators. They had stopped on the third floor. Maintenance was in a room off to the side of the lobby, and Brigham poked his head into their break room. One of the janitors, Ali, was there. A little over a year ago, Brigham himself had been a janitor before he passed the Bar exam.

"Ali, how's it hanging?" Brigham knew he loved that

expression, and it always made him smile widely.

"I saw you on TV," Ali said. "How can a man do that to his friend's hat?"

"Revenge makes people do sick things, I guess. Hey, do you have a ladder?"

Brigham held the ladder while Ali retrieved the balloon. He handed it to Brigham and said, "How's it hanging?"

"No, you only say it as a greeting, not as a goodbye."

"Oh. I still like it."

Brigham rode the elevator up to the accounting firm on the third floor. The secretary was busy on the phone, so he just walked past her and saw the boy and his father in a large glass-walled conference room with three other people. Brigham entered, and they all stared at him. He sheepishly handed the balloon to the boy.

"My balloon!"

"Have a good one," Brigham said as he left. He glanced over his shoulder, and they were still staring at him as he returned to the elevator.

The offices of Theodore, Becker & Sheffield occupied a nice corner on the seventh floor overlooking Main Street and the Zions Bank across the street. Brigham walked in to the sound of people speaking on phones, faxes coming through, and clients talking in the waiting room. He had to stop a moment and just enjoy it. This was a real firm. A real law firm that they had built with nothing.

After passing the Bar a year and a half ago, he'd worked for a man called Tommy Two-Balls, who was killed. Brigham never knew why. When he, Molly, and Scotty decided to open their own firm, none of them knew what was going to happen. The unknown was one of the most frightening things to face. But it had worked. He'd won his first real case, which had been a black mark for Vince Dale, the senior trial prosecutor, now the Salt Lake County district attorney. They advertised a little on the internet and had done a couple of radio spots on the hard rock and rap stations, but word of mouth had been the amazing advertising tool everyone had told him it could be.

As he rounded the corner from the waiting room, Scotty accosted him. His broad shoulders would have looked better if he'd had the height to go with them, but instead, he was short and round. A Scottish accent had stuck with him, though he tried desperately to shed it.

"Brigham, we need to talk about hiring more people," he said, following him through the hall.

"We will."

"I'm swamped. I've got over eighty cases on my plate. I need help."

"I know, we're all swamped. I promise, Scotty, we'll hire a couple of people."

"Well, I'm hiring a new paralegal right now—a girl at the

coffee shop who always gives me a free pastry."

"Fine, done."

As Scotty left, one of the paralegals, Lexi, ran up to him with a stack of documents. She shoved a pen into his hand and held them as he scribbled his name on them. "And don't forget you have a consult at seven," she said.

"Why so late?"

"That's the only time they could make it."

Another one of his paralegals saw him and made a beeline for him before he ducked into Molly's office. He shut the door behind him and took a breath. Molly stopped typing and looked up at him.

"How'd it go?" she asked.

"No jail."

"Really? I thought they wouldn't offer that."

"He was attacked by the hat's owner and the prosecutor didn't want a mistrial."

"Well, good job. That case got some press."

He shrugged and went over to kiss her lightly on the lips before sitting down across from her. "Dinner tonight?"

"You name the place," she said, turning back to her computer.

"What's going on with the chi mo?"

"Our client *accused* of child molestation will be going to trial in a week. You don't use the words 'accused' or 'allegedly'

13

enough."

"I'm joking."

"Well, joke somewhere else, please. I've got work to do."

Brigham rose and kissed her again before leaving and shutting the door. In his office, he found a skinny man with a puff of white hair on his head sitting in the chair in front of his desk: his accountant, Martin.

"Don't you guys ever make appointments?" Brigham said, sitting down.

"I have access to all your money. You sure you want to be givin' me lip?"

"I'm sorry, dear sweet Martin. To what do I owe the wonderful pleasure of your company?"

He grinned. "Smart-ass." Martin opened a file and set it on the desk. "Your balance sheet. You guys are doing well and everything's stable right now, but it won't last. Word of mouth only gets you so far. You've got to advertise more."

"Advertise where?"

"I represent several law firms, and the others are all doing everything. Billboards, radio, TV, internet—there's a ton of places to go. Invest in advertising as much as you can so we keep these numbers up. I'd also expand into other areas, like small claims or bankruptcy."

"I hate that stuff," Brigham said, flipping through the papers in the file.

"So hire someone else to do it. The more diversity you have, the more stable you'll be if one particular field dries up. And for crap's sake, you're the hot young lawyer in town right now, so get yourself some better suits."

"What's wrong with my suits?"

"You bought them secondhand and they don't fit. My tailor's up the street, Roberto. He'll take good care of you."

Martin rose, gazing out the windows. "You know, I was Tommy's accountant for twelve years. Bastard never missed a birthday or anniversary. There was always a gift in the mail, usually cash. A joke, because he was always trying to keep money off the books by being paid in cash, and I would always argue with him about it. I miss him."

Brigham nodded. "I do, too."

"Well, keep up the good fight."

Martin left, and Brigham was alone with a stack of files. He had more than seventy active criminal cases right now, about half of them drug or alcohol related. It amazed him that the government spent so much time and money fighting things as innocuous as steroids and marijuana. He had always thought that prosecuting innocuous things degraded the whole justice system. People knew marijuana wasn't that harmful—nowhere near as dangerous as cigarettes or alcohol. And because the government prosecuted marijuana cases so aggressively, people—particularly the younger generations—began to wonder whether all the laws weren't ridiculous. How could you respect the rule of law when it was so wrong about something?

Brigham began going through the files, making notes in the margins of police reports. Most were run of the mill. Reasonable suspicion—the reason for police contact with the defendant—and probable cause—the reason the police arrested and searched the defendant—were the two standard challenges in any drug or alcohol case, particularly DUIs. He separated his DUI files and found that he had twenty active DUIs, meaning cases that weren't going to settle, and almost all of them needed motions drafted. Scotty was right; he would need to hire somebody. He went online and began writing an ad.

After five minutes, all he had was, "Downtown Salt Lake City law firm seeks associate attorney. Must be comfortable in court."

He couldn't really think of anything else that was important to him. Attention to detail didn't matter, since the paralegals were the ones keeping track of deadlines and court dates. Neither did punctuality, or grades, or any of the other things new lawyers thought were important. Criminal defense attorneys nationwide lost three quarters of their trials. The prosecution had all the evidence and offered good deals or dismissed their bad cases, which meant the ones going to trial were usually the worst cases for the defense. The only thing he wanted in an associate was someone who could talk to a jury in a way that made them see the defendant as a human being.

The door opened, and Scotty wandered in. He sat down and didn't look at Brigham right away. Instead, he had his face buried in his iPad. "I need you to do something for me," he said eventually.

"What?"

"Go to the Salt Lake Justice Court on a DUI."

"Why? What's going on with it?"

"Nathaniel's the prosecutor. He never gives me anything. I don't think he respects me."

"Maybe it's a dog case."

He shook his head. "No, we have something. Bad stop. They said she was weaving between lanes. The cop didn't actually see her cross the white lines. He heard it from a third-party witness, who they didn't get any information on. But Nathaniel's just not giving me a deal."

"I'm sure he has a reason."

Scotty looked up, his eyes widening and narrowing again in a tic Brigham had seen before. "People decide things based on their guts and then look for reasons to justify it. So his guts told him not to give me a deal, and he's found some bullshit reason for it. I need you to go. He likes you."

Brigham posted the ad on several sites and then stood up. He would rather be in a courtroom than the office any day. "Get me the file."

3

Every city in Utah had a justice court. The city kept the fines collected from defendants whose cases were handled by the justice court rather than losing the money to the county or the state. But the trade-off was that justice courts could only handle low-level misdemeanors. The most serious cases they handled were minor domestic violence cases and DUIs. Also, anything from the justice court could be appealed to the higher, county-wide district court, which meant defense attorneys got two tries for an acquittal.

The Salt Lake City Justice Court sat between a run-down apartment building and a mechanic's shop. As Brigham went through the metal detectors, he realized nothing that happened here really mattered. Every decision made here could be appealed to the district court, and the case started over again. In a way, it was liberating. Lawyers could try things here they would never dream of trying in front of a district court.

Brigham was pulled aside to be wanded by one of the bailiffs. He knew the day they stopped doing that, the day they actually recognized that he was here at least once a week, was the day he would truly have made it as a lawyer.

He ran up the stairs to the second level and flipped through the file one more time. Jessica Padilla was accused of DUI and possession of marijuana. Scotty had been correct; the stop wasn't good. The cop claimed there had been an anonymous tipster but took no information from him. By the time the DUI investigation was done, the tipster was gone. A video, according to Scotty, showed she hadn't been weaving between the lanes and no one other than the cop had seen or talked to the tipster.

The courtroom was packed, and people were even standing in the back. Brigham crossed the courtroom and headed straight for the prosecution table. Nathaniel sat with his back straight, making notes in his files, waiting for the judge.

"Hey," Brigham said.

"Brigham, what's up, man?"

"Nothing much," Brigham said, taking a seat next to him. "How's life as a bureaucrat?"

"I wish I was a bureaucrat. I'm just a cog in a big, giant wheel, man."

"Well, you're one of the better cogs if that helps."

"Not really, but thanks. Who you here on?"

"Jessica Padilla."

Nathaniel was quiet a moment. "Sorry, man. No offers on that one."

"Just like that? Have you looked at the stop?"

"I have. But this comes from on high."

"On high as in…?"

"The highest of highs."

"Ah. Any particular reason?"

Nathaniel shrugged, scanning the table before pulling out a yellow file. He opened it and showed Brigham the notes on the inside flap. "See for yourself."

Scrawled across the notes section was a single sentence: NO DEALS ON THIS CASE. Underneath the sentence were the initials GH—Gwen Henries, the chief prosecutor.

"She usually do that?" Brigham asked.

"Not really. Your girl must've really done something to tick her off."

Brigham nodded. "Gwen over there right now?"

"Yup. Have fun."

"Thanks." Brigham rose and faced the audience. "Jessica Padilla?" he bellowed.

An attractive young woman in a top that exposed her shoulders stood up. He hurried down the aisle and led her outside the courtroom so they could speak.

"Hey, I'm Brigham. I work with Scotty."

"Oh, okay," she said. "Nice to meet you."

"You, too. So I had a quick question: do you know Gwen Henries?"

She thought a moment. "No, I don't think so."

"She's kinda short, blond hair, went to law school at UCLA."

"Doesn't sound familiar, no."

"Hm. Okay, well, have a seat in the courtroom. I'll be right back."

The Salt Lake City Prosecutor's Office was one building away from the justice court. The city had seventeen prosecutors with double that in staff, and it was widely recognized that they were a recruiting ground for the district attorney's office. Most people at the DA's office began their careers in the city and cut their teeth on misdemeanors. People didn't notice screw ups on misdemeanors.

Brigham hurried up the sidewalk and into the building. It had no security guard, probably because of budget cuts, and he rode the elevator to the fifth floor. Stepping out, he saw the prosecutor's offices took up the entire floor. A young girl sat behind protective glass at the entrance.

"Hi, I'm an attorney, Brigham Theodore. I was wondering if I could talk to Gwen for just a second?"

"Hang on, I'll see if she's in."

The receptionist said something into her phone that Brigham couldn't hear and then turned to him and said, "Come on in."

A locked door clicked open, and he stepped through some metal detectors inside. No bailiff was there to wand him, and the receptionist didn't say anything, so he wandered around the offices looking for Gwen Henries.

The offices were small and so close together that he was certain each prosecutor could hear exactly what the ones next door were doing. Down the hall he saw Gwen's name on the door of the corner office. He knocked and stuck his head around the corner. She saw him but didn't smile.

"Mr. Theodore, what can I do for you?"

Brigham sat down without being asked, and she looked annoyed by it. He cleared his throat. "You made a note not to give any offers to a client of mine, and I was hoping I could talk you out of that."

"What client is that?"

"Jessica Padilla."

"Oh, her," she said, leaning back in the chair. "Yes, I did make that note."

"Can I ask why?"

"Sure you can."

Brigham grinned though he felt annoyed. "*May* I ask why?"

"You may."

"Why did you make that note, Gwen?"

"Because your client is an alcoholic and needs severe punishment. A slap on the wrist won't do it. So you can plead or go to trial."

"Her BAC wasn't that high. She was barely over the legal limit. And it might be a bad stop. Why the tough stance?"

"I told you," she said, turning back to her computer. "She's dangerous."

Brigham got the impression that the conversation was over. *No biggie*. He'd be glad to take it to trial. He stood and said, "Thanks for your time."

"No problem," she said without looking up.

When he got back to court, the judge had already taken the bench. He waited his turn. When he got up to the lectern, he said, "Your Honor, may we call the matter of Jessica Padilla, please?"

"Certainly. Ms. Padilla, please come forward… okay, Counsel, what are we doing on this?"

"We'd like to set this for a motion to suppress based on a lack of reasonable suspicion for the stop."

"You got it. Thirty days enough? Two weeks to get the motion in and two weeks for the response if there is any?"

"That's fine, thank you. If I may be excused, Your Honor."

Brigham calendared the new date with the judge's clerk and left the building. Once they were outside, he turned to Jessica and said, "You sure you don't know Gwen?"

She shook her head. "I'm not sure. But I really don't think so."

He nodded. "Well, just be here next time and we'll see if we can get this taken care of."

As he headed to his bike—he hadn't bought a car yet—he wondered why Gwen had been so weird about the whole thing. He'd met her several times before and had been up against her for a few trials. She'd never taken a stance she couldn't explain well.

Brigham thought about heading home but remembered he had a consult coming in at seven. He turned his bike around and headed back to the office.

4

Molly Becker sat at her desk and drafted a motion in limine, a document asking the judge to order certain evidence to be kept out of trial, in preparation for her trial next week. Court was a comfortable place for her. She'd begun her career in a big firm doing divorces and corporate law, which required a solid amount of court time. And not just court time but time dealing with intense and emotional disagreements. Neither side was ever happy in a divorce, and both clients always blamed their attorneys. She remembered one case vividly in which she had completely lost the hearing, but the opposing side yelled at his attorney after court because he thought he had lost. Divorces were a lose-lose situation. Criminal law was much more fun.

The intercom on her phone buzzed. "Yeah?"

"Lee Olsen here for his appointment," the receptionist said.

"Send him back, please."

She finished her sentence and then leaned back in her chair, waiting for Olsen. When he walked in, he smiled widely. He looked like someone who coached tennis lessons, not someone who was on trial for child rape.

As they shook hands, a twinge of revulsion went through her, but she pushed it out of her mind and took her seat. "How are you, Lee?"

"I've been better. Whadya need to see me for?"

"I wanted to talk to you in person. This is going to be the last chance you have to take a plea deal. When we show up for trial on Wednesday, that's it. We have to go through with it at that point."

"So, run through the deal again?"

"You'll be pleading to one count of sexual abuse of a child and doing one to fifteen in prison. It also comes with a lifetime sex-offender registration. But if we go to trial and lose, you're looking at twenty-five to life."

He smirked. "Up to fifteen years in prison and life as a sex offender? No thanks. I'll take my chances."

"You sure? Because after today—"

"I'm sure."

She nodded. "Okay, well, make sure you wear a suit on Wednesday and be there at eight a.m. sharp."

He nodded and left without another word. Most clients wanted to chitchat, but he was all business, which Molly actually preferred. She sighed and turned to her computer, staring at the words of the motion. They were just words, dead letters on a page. The case itself involved a real person—a young boy who had gone through hell. His fate, and Lee's, were now just words on a page.

She leaned her head back, allowing her sore neck to rest for a second, and then began writing again.

5

The offices were nearly empty by the time Brigham returned. He walked back to his office and worked on his inbox for a while before he heard the door to their suite open. The cleaning staff usually didn't come in until eight, so he went to the door.

A middle-aged man stood there, wearing a maroon sweater though it was probably seventy degrees out. He had his hands in his pockets and a melancholy expression that seemed to preclude him looking up.

Brigham went over to him and asked, "Ted Montgomery?"

"Yes."

"Brigham Theodore. Nice to meet you. Come on back to my office."

Brigham sat down at his desk, and Ted sat across from him, looking uncomfortable, fidgeting, and not meeting Brigham's eyes. Something about him seemed familiar.

"Have we met before?" Brigham said.

"No."

Brigham pulled out a legal pad and a pen. He wrote "TED MONTGOMERY" across the top. "So what can I do for you?"

"I was referred to you by a colleague. He said you defended his daughter on a drug charge and were amazing. I'm facing a charge right now myself."

"What is the charge?"

"Murder."

Brigham started to write the charge down, then stopped. He hadn't had a murder case since his first a year ago. His eyes darted up to Ted's. The man had soft eyes, something like a deer—no malice or conniving in them. "That's where I've seen you, isn't it? A photo on a news website."

He nodded. "My story got some press, yes."

"I just glanced at the headline. What're you accused of doing?"

He glanced down again, his fingers interlaced on his lap. "It was my wife." He swallowed. "Ruby Montgomery. She had pancreatic cancer. She didn't have much longer left, and it's nearly one hundred percent fatal. She asked that… I just didn't want her to suffer anymore."

Brigham leaned forward, his elbows on the desk. "What did you do?"

"It's called managed death. I read about it online. The doctors are not allowed to take her life, but they can turn up her pain medication to doses that would be considered… risky. We were there, her family, and we turned the morphine as high as I thought necessary. She passed shortly after, quietly, surrounded by her family. I was brought in for questioning a couple of hours later, but I snuck away before they could arrest me. I think I have a warrant out now."

A memory flashed in Brigham's mind. The pain of it shot through him, and he swallowed it down, pushing it as far away from his conscious thoughts as he could. "How much is the bail on the warrant for?"

"I don't know."

Brigham turned to his computer. He opened the database for statewide warrants and ran Ted's name through. He was charged in Salt Lake County District Court with first-degree homicide. The bail on the warrant out for his arrest was half a million dollars.

"You would need fifty thousand to bail out right now, plus some collateral. I might be able to get that lowered. We need to go to court and start the process. You'll have to turn yourself in."

He nodded. "I figured. I just wanted to talk to you first."

"Ted, did you discuss everything with the doctors first?"

"Until I was blue in the face. They said there was nothing they could do. She was going to die, it was just a matter of time. But they couldn't make her comfortable. The pain was just too much. They wouldn't do anything, so I did. I got the morphine and I put it into her drip. It was very quiet, her passing."

Tears came to his eyes, and a twinge of pain must've gone

through him because he grimaced.

Brigham didn't say anything for a while. He just let Ted gather himself before asking, "How old was she?"

"Thirty-nine. Just a kid. Ten years younger than me. We have three kids. They were there with her when…"

Brigham nodded. Under the ethical rules of any Bar in the country, a criminal lawyer was not allowed to advise a client to run, but he couldn't keep it inside him. As carefully as he could, he said, "If convicted, you could be facing life in prison. Are you sure you want to do this?"

He nodded. "My kids are here, and my career. I'm too old to start over in Croatia or Mexico. I can't leave my kids here on their own. My youngest is only five."

"Then we need to have you booked. I'll go down to the jail with you."

He nodded. "You can name your fee. My father is paying for everything. I'll give you his number."

Brigham rose then remembered he didn't have a car. "Meet me down there in an hour," he said.

The Salt Lake County Metro Jail was a gray and beige cube with no obvious entrances or exits. The only entrance was up a ramp and around a corner, hidden from view as if they were discouraging people from finding it.

Brigham locked his bike up in front of the entrance, and through two sets of glass doors, he saw Ted Montgomery. He was sitting in the waiting room in front of a row of deputies and clerks who controlled who entered the jail and when. He was staring absently at the linoleum. Next to him were three children: two teenagers and a young boy who was holding Ted's hand. Brigham entered and sat next to them.

"Your kids?" Brigham asked.

"Yes. This is Monica, Devan, and David."

Brigham smiled at them, unsure what to say. Monica was the oldest, probably sixteen or seventeen, and had makeup running down her face. Her eyes were rimmed red. Devan was staring at the floor, and the youngest, David, was kicking his legs, his feet unable to reach the ground from the chair.

"You ready?" Brigham said.

Ted nodded. He turned to Monica and wrapped his arms around her. Without a sound, her body convulsed, and tears rolled down Ted's cheeks as he whispered, "I'll be okay."

Devan wouldn't look up. His eyes were glued to the floor until his father put his hand underneath his chin and raised the older boy's eyes to his. "You're the man of the house while I'm gone. You take good care of these two. Okay?"

He nodded but didn't say anything.

Ted kissed his forehead then put his arms around his youngest son, David. The boy wrapped his arms around his father, and they held each other for a moment—long enough that Monica hugged her father again.

Brigham had to look away. He gave them as long as they needed, until Ted said, "Okay."

Brigham walked to the first clerk. "Brigham Theodore. I'm here with my client, Ted Montgomery. He'd like to surrender."

As Ted was cuffed and taken to the back for processing, Brigham watched his children. They held onto each other tightly, all three crying now. Monica hugged the other two and said, "Daddy will be home soon."

Brigham watched as Ted kept his eyes on his children until the deputy dragged him around a corner, and he was gone.

6

Friday mornings at the Salt Lake County DA's office were reserved for team meetings. Debra Flynn had been there for six years and, if there were anything she could change about her job, it would be the meetings.

The meetings took place in a massive conference room with the team leader at the front and all the frontline prosecutors around him. Bagels and coffee were served, and that day, she got a bagel, bit into it, and set it on a napkin before pushing it away from her. The bagel was stale and hard, probably left over from another meeting.

While there were multiple teams, covering everything from juvenile crime to murder and high-profile cases, she was already in the high-profile section despite being one of the younger attorneys in the office at thirty-two. "High profile" meant cases that had attracted media attention, and the DA, Vince Dale, wanted any case that received media attention to get the proper treatment—specifically, the result had to make him look good.

Debra had won several felony trials and then a capital murder before Vince recruited her for that section. During the meeting, he had said, "I want extensions of myself in the HP section." She hadn't understood what that meant and still didn't. She did her job the best she could and let everything else take care of itself.

Her team leader was Johnny Presto. When she'd first met him, she'd thought that was his nickname, but it was his real name. Johnny flipped through a few things on his iPad and said, "Okay, we got three cases to split this morning. Tammy, you're up—you got a rape of a legislator's wife at a frat party. What the hell she was doing at a frat party I don't know, but the legislator has been meeting with Vince three or four times a month and is becoming a pain in his ass. Make it go away and keep the legislator as happy as possible. Colby, we got Farmington's mayor's son busted on a DUI. Vince wants to make sure we treat everybody equally and doesn't want any special considerations for the son. Treat him like every other DUI."

Debra grinned to herself as she looked out the windows. Equality didn't exist for Vince Dale. The mayor of Farmington had thrown his support behind Vince's opponent in this year's election. If he hadn't, she was certain Johnny would be giving some different instructions.

"Debbie, we got something for you: murder of a cancer patient at the U of U Hospital. Killed by her husband. Juicy stuff. Vince wants full bore on this one. The guy killed her in the hospital in front of her children."

"Shit," someone said.

"Yeah," Johnny said without looking up from the iPad. "Fry his ass, Deb."

"I'll do my best."

The meeting consisted of a few other items. The frontline prosecutors were expected to "staff" cases, meaning discuss them with everyone, where they were considering making a plea deal that might be too good for the defense. Several people brought up their cases, but Debra didn't have any of those.

When the meeting was over, she went back to her office. On the way, Colby came up to her. "That case sounds fun."

"Which one?"

"Yours. The murder."

"Oh. Sounds like a lotta work actually. I'll trade you if you want."

He shook his head. "No way. DUI where I get to roast a mayor's son? Any day. Plus it'll be almost no work on my part."

She stopped in front of her office. "They wouldn't let me trade anyway."

"Why not?"

She shook her head. "Just lucky, I guess."

"Well, kick ass. Son of a bitch doesn't deserve any compassion if he did that in front of his kids."

"Don't worry, he won't get any from me."

Debra's shift, if you could call it that, consisted of half a day of paperwork and half a day of courtroom time. The courtroom, at least for her, was a place to relax. The office was where she felt the most stress and pressure. Court was her realm. She sat in the jury box as cases were called and read a trashy romance novel—something about a pirate kidnapping the daughter of a governor and the two falling in love.

Only one of her eight cases that day was set for trial. Few defense attorneys liked trial, in her experience. The reasons were probably that some were scared and didn't like losing, and some thought it wasn't profitable. For the prep time and then two or three days, or worse, weeks, of trial when they couldn't do anything else, they were losing money. If most solo defense attorneys were barely making it as it was, a long trial could bankrupt them if they didn't charge enough for it.

Of all the cases she had, the one that was set for trial was the one with the youngest attorney—a kid who looked like he had just graduated from high school. The case was a theft in which his client—the husband of a CEO with ties to the state Democratic party—was accused of stealing another man's wallet while at the customer service counter at Walmart. After the attorney had set it for trial, Debra followed him out into the hall.

"Excuse me. Can we talk for a sec?"

The attorney said to his client, "Call me if you have any questions," and then walked over. "You ready to offer us that deal?" the attorney asked.

"The opposite. You're going to go back into that courtroom, cancel the trial, and set it for disposition so your client can plead guilty. Doesn't matter what the sentence is going to be. That's just what you're going to do."

He snorted. "And why would I do that?"

"Because your client's sister is here illegally. My next call is to ICE, and they're going to happen to pop into her work to pay her a visit. If he pleads guilty, no deportation for the sister. If he makes me do the trial, she's getting deported whether I win or lose."

The attorney's face contorted in anger, and a flush painted his cheeks. Debra didn't move her eyes; she kept them fixed on him and stayed cool, almost passive. She had learned that people who lost their tempers seemed to grow angrier when she kept her emotions in check.

"Why would you be such a bitch?"

She took a step closer to him. "You just added a thousand dollars to his fine. Keep talking and I'll add more."

"You can't punish him for what I said!"

"I can and will. And then guess what? Maybe I'll talk to the other prosecutors at the DA's office about what you just called me. Maybe you'll find that you just can't get a good deal for any of your clients in Salt Lake County anymore."

He shook his head and didn't move for a while then finally brushed past her and went back into the courtroom.

She grinned and headed back to the office to pick up her things.

7

Brigham stood by the windows in his office, staring down at the street. It was late in the evening, and his day had been packed with client meetings and court hearings. He'd lost a motion to suppress on a drug case but won a sentencing argument, keeping his client out of jail on an assault case. He should have felt good, but instead he had a tight knot in his gut.

Molly knocked on his open door. He glanced back at her and gave her a melancholy grin before turning back to the window.

"Heard you signed up Ted Montgomery. That's a great case. It's all over the news."

He shook his head but didn't turn around. "I don't know if I'm going to take it."

She was silent for a moment. "May I ask why?"

"He killed this woman in front of her children."

"That's one interpretation. The other is that he saved her from months of pain that would have left them motherless anyway."

"Maybe. I don't know."

She crossed the room and stood next to him. "Well,

whatever you decide is fine by me. I just came to tell you your interview's here."

"What interview?"

"For another attorney. I'll send her back."

When Molly left, Brigham watched a bicyclist rush across the intersection and nearly get clipped by a car.

The office seemed claustrophobic today, as if it were closing in around him. He wanted to go for a walk, but just as he was about to head out and tell Scotty to do the interview, Molly was back with the applicant.

The young woman wore glasses and a black suit with a Tibetan flag pin on her lapel.

"Brigham, this is Rebecca Cruz. Rebecca, Brigham."

"Good to meet you," she said, pushing up her glasses. She sat down and Brigham sat across from her.

"Do you have your resumé?" he asked.

"You don't care about my resumé."

"I don't?"

"No. All your ad said was that you had to be comfortable in court, so I didn't think you would care about what my grades were and stuff like that."

"You're right. I don't."

"So I brought something else instead. An argument. It's the closing I gave in my trial ad class."

He leaned back in his chair. "Let's see it."

42

"It's a prostitution case. They gave me an impossible case to win because my client, the prostitute, was caught in the act."

Rebecca stood up and adjusted her suit. She closed her eyes a moment and then took a deep breath. "Nasreen Boyce is not guilty of this crime. She's not a pimp. Because that's what they're accusing her of—being a pimp. The government wants you to believe that Nasreen posts ads for her and her friends online and then meets men for sex. Well, look at that ad. Tell me where on that ad it says anything about sex. It says that they give massages. And I get that some of you may be thinking, 'well, that's just a cover.' But it's not a cover. It's what they do. These are girls who come from horrific backgrounds and have very few ways to support themselves.

"My client has been on her own since she was thirteen. Her stepfather was abusive and threw her into the street when she would no longer succumb to his advances. She had to find a way to survive. But even though she starved, she never once prostituted herself. Not once. I introduced her criminal record to you when she took the stand. From the age of thirteen until now, there were never, ever any charges for prostitution or pimping. Why? Because that's not what she does. She discovered early that you didn't need sex to make money. A massage was enough. And that's how she makes her living. Unlike these Vice detectives.

"Did you notice that they got naked, came into the room,

talked dirty to her, and then let her massage them? You listened to them testify about what happened. Well, I disagree with what they say happened, as does my client. An easy way to prove who's right would be to record these encounters. They transmitted the sound through cell phones they left on, which other detectives were listening to, but they stopped recording them.

"Why did they stop recording them? Because they don't want you to hear what happened. They want you to take their word for it. Well, that's not good enough. This is the United States of America in the twenty-first century. We are not Salem five hundred years ago, where we're burning witches at the stake because some people are pointing the finger. And ask yourselves, other than finger-pointing from these two detectives who refused to record the encounter, what other evidence is there? What great proof do they have that my client is a pimp and a prostitute? Nothing. They don't have anything. And that's the magic act the prosecution is trying to pull: making something from nothing. Don't let them. Don't let them burn people who they think are witches. Tell them if they want a conviction, then they need real proof… which they just don't have in this case."

Rebecca adjusted her glasses and sat back down.

Brigham grinned at her. "You're hired."

8

After setting Rebecca up with one of the paralegals to get her new-hire paperwork started, Brigham headed out. The girl was decent—some rough edges, but she hit on the right points. She brought up the United States of America—which tapped a patriotic nerve—she kept saying the prosecution was accusing her client of being a pimp, forcing the jury to think in her terms rather than the government's—not a tactic Brigham totally agreed with, as he thought a jury could see through misdirection from a mile away, but clever nonetheless—and she lambasted them for not recording the incident. With a little experience, she was going to be really good.

The sun was fading by the time he stepped out of the building. The sunset here had a different flavor than in his native Louisiana. It had a more sweeping grandeur, as though the mountains bounced the light and lit everything up, not just the sky.

He took the inner-city train, Trax, back to his apartment, trying to make up his mind. Even the thought of another murder case tired him. The preparation hours were brutal. The trial would only be a handful of days, a week or two at the most, but the prep time could be enormous. It would suck up all of his time. And he didn't know if he wanted to defend Ted.

The Trax stopped near his building and he got off. In his old place, rent had been cheaper than groceries, but now he could afford somewhere a little better. At least better enough that there weren't cockroaches, and he didn't worry about people breaking in and robbing him.

He opened his door on the second floor and flopped on his couch then slipped his shoes off, staring at the ceiling. Hunger pangs pounded in his stomach, but eating was too much effort; all his strength was going to blocking some memories he didn't want brought back.

His phone buzzed in his pocket and he took it out. It was the office. "This is Brigham."

"Hey, this is Rebecca. You just hired me."

"I remember. What can I do for you?"

"I just wanted to say thanks. You took off before I could, so I called."

"No problem," he said. "I'm sure you'll do great."

"I heard you're doing the Ted Montgomery case—I just saw a clip about it on KSL."

"Well, I don't know if we're taking it, actually."

"Why not?"

"I don't know. A bunch of reasons, I guess."

"I feel bad for those kids. They just lost their mom and

46

now they might lose their dad, too. If you can do anything for him, I would be happy to help."

Brigham knew she was right; they had already lost one parent only to see the other one hauled away in handcuffs. "Yeah, thanks."

"Okay, well, I'll see you tomorrow."

"Tomorrow."

Brigham hung up and tapped the phone against his palm. He rose, got his shoes, and headed out the door again.

The address Ted Montgomery had listed as his home on the new-client paperwork was only a thirty-minute train ride away. Brigham got there just after dark. The lights were on inside the home, and he stood on the sidewalk for a second and just watched. A television spread flickering blue light inside. He took a deep breath, crossed the lawn to the front porch, and knocked.

Monica, the oldest, answered.

"Hi," Brigham said.

"Hi," she said shyly. "You're Dad's lawyer, right?"

"Um, yeah. Yeah, I just wanted to come check on you guys."

"You can come in."

Brigham hesitated. He didn't know exactly what he was

doing here or why he had come, but going inside hadn't been his plan. Regardless, he followed her in.

The front room was cluttered, mostly toys and children's books, but it wasn't dirty. Devan, the middle child, sat on the couch and stared blankly at the television. David was off somewhere else, but Brigham could hear him making car or airplane noises.

"No one's staying with you guys?" Brigham asked.

She shook her head. "We don't have anyone else. We're from Oregon and don't have any family here." She crossed her arms, looking over at her brother. "I wish we'd stayed in Oregon."

"Why'd you move?"

"My dad got a new job. We were only here, like, a couple of months before my mom got sick."

Brigham saw David run through the kitchen, a toy airplane in his hand. "How are you paying the bills?"

"My dad left an account for me. It should last a year. And then I guess I have to get a job."

Brigham looked around the house. He knew that the Department of Child and Family Services would be notified. They would likely take all three of them and place them in foster care—temporary at first, but then permanently if Ted was convicted and sent to prison. He didn't have the heart to tell her that yet.

She stared at her brother a moment and then said, "Do you want to see my mom?"

Brigham nodded, unsure what she meant. Monica walked into the kitchen, and he followed her. She took her cell phone and then connected it to a desktop in the corner, and an image came up.

It was clearly taken on a phone poking around the corner, facing a hospital bed. Standing next to the bed was Ted Montgomery. In the bed was a woman.

She was nearly bald, with sporadic puffs of hair on her head and strands on the pillow. The woman was pale, colorless and white, and thin as a pole. She was crying, and Ted was crying, too, holding her hand.

"Please," she said quietly, "I can't anymore... I just can't. It hurts so much... It hurts so much."

Ted kissed her on the forehead. "I know. You just have to hang on."

"No," she said, sobbing. "Please, Ted, do something. Do something!"

"I... I can't."

The two of them held each other, weeping into each other's arms. The phone was pulled out of the room and the video ended.

"That was a month before she died," Monica said solemnly. "I took it. I took a lot of videos of her in the hospital.

Dad said I should, so I could remember her when she was gone."

Brigham swallowed. He wasn't sure what to say, so he said nothing for a long time. Monica's eyes were glued to the screen as she rewound the video and stopped on an image of her mother and father hugging.

"I'm sorry, Monica. I'm so sorry you had to go through this."

"Can you help my dad?"

Brigham hesitated. "I don't know."

She looked back at the screen. "My mom always told me that people suffer for a reason. God has a plan for them. What's the reason He did this to us? Devan's nine years old. He doesn't eat or sleep. In school, he just sits there and doesn't do any work or talk to anybody." She looked back at him again. "Why would God do this to him? He's never hurt anybody in his life."

Brigham shook his head. "I don't know."

"I know my dad doesn't mean anything to you. But he was there for my mom for a year while she died. He gave up everything he had to take care of her. He doesn't have anyone to take care of him now. Except you. Please take care of him."

Brigham nodded as David ran by them, sliding the airplane against the wall. "I will," he said. "I promise."

9

Jury selection, or *voir dire*, had gone quickly. Molly didn't put much stock in it. A little more than Brigham did, but still not much. She asked a few broad questions and made certain no one on the jury panel had been a victim of sexual abuse or had relatives or friends that had been. Other than that, she tried to strike those who went to church frequently and registered as Republicans. Liberals, in her view, tended to acquit more frequently.

In the end, the eight-person jury consisted of three women and five men. All except two had gone to college, and none of them had any criminal charges. In her estimation, it was about as good as she was going to get in Salt Lake County.

The case was before Judge Veasman, a pudgy man who seemed to be asleep most of the time during trials. He looked to the prosecutor after the jury was impaneled and said, "All yours."

The prosecutor was a man Molly knew well—Kevin Renteria. They had even dated briefly. Kevin buttoned his top jacket button as he rose and sauntered toward the jury. He stood with his hands behind his back and looked at each juror before speaking.

"On September the fifth of last year, Lee Olsen"—he turned and pointed to Lee, who was seated next to Molly—"did something so horrific that it's difficult to wrap your mind around. He walked into his sister's house on Fourth West and Twenty-First South in Salt Lake and saw that no one was home except his little nephew, Michael Olsen. Michael was watching television, not paying attention to his uncle. Lee had been over so often that there was no reason to be alarmed that he was there by himself. Even if Michael was just ten years old, it wasn't unusual."

Kevin took a step to the right so he could meet the eyes of the jurors on the other side of the box. "Michael was sitting on the couch. Lee sat next to him. He talked to him for a few minutes, putting the boy at ease, and then began rubbing his leg. He moved up the thigh until he came to Michael's genitals. And then he began rubbing them. It lasted a few minutes, but Michael will tell you it felt even longer. And then this man forced Michael down onto the couch, stripped off his shorts and his underwear, and raped him. No lubrication was used. The boy was sodomized so violently that he required twenty stitches in his rectum. But Michael didn't fight... This was his uncle." Kevin stepped closer to the jury and put his hands on the jury box. "His uncle. Who he loved and trusted and had known his entire life. And there he was on top of him, raping him."

Kevin looked to Lee and his lip curled in disgust.

"This man, or whatever he is, ruined this boy's life. He took away everything Michael was going to be and do. Michael's life was going one way, and now it will be going another because he"—Kevin pointed to Lee again—"saw vulnerability and exploited it. He saw his chance and took it." He turned back to the jury. "Michael didn't do anything to deserve something like this. He is completely and utterly innocent—a true innocent: just a child. He was forced to endure the most painful, humiliating thing a person can endure, and the worst part of it was that he had been close to his Uncle Lee. They were buddies. They played sports together. Lee would bring him gifts if he traveled anywhere. Lee taught him about camping and fishing and how to throw a football with a spiral and a million other things. How is Michael ever supposed to trust anyone again? How is he supposed to find solace in life?"

Kevin took a few paces back. "You let Lee Olsen know he doesn't get to do that and get away with it. He doesn't get to rape children and then turn himself in with a smile as though nothing had happened. Find him guilty, and show him that we live in a society of law—law that doesn't allow you to rape the most innocent among us, and get away with it.

Kevin sat back down and undid the top button of his suit

coat again. Molly stood up, and as she walked past Lee to get to the jury, she set her hand on his shoulder as a signal to the jury that he wasn't a monster, that he wasn't dangerous. If a skinny blonde wasn't afraid of him, maybe they had no reason to be, either.

"It's true that Lee was over at his sister's house that day. It's true that Michael was in the home. But it's not true that Lee did anything to Michael. Lee loves his family and would do anything to protect them. He works a job he hates for twelve hours a day in order to provide for his wife and unborn child. He's got a full-time job as a house painter and has picked up another part-time one for auto repair. He is a man who has a lot of compassion and intelligence. He's a man who wouldn't do this."

She walked back over to the defense table and leaned on it. She had to be careful about this portion. Utah had some of the strictest rape-shield laws in the country, so she was not allowed to mention anything about prior bad acts by the victim. But there was an exception to the rape shield: if a prior sexual encounter could explain something in the current case, it should be allowed in.

"Semen was found on the victim, both on the front, near his genitals, and in his rectum. That semen was tested for genetic identity, and guess what? It is not a match to Lee Olsen. Lee was literally begging to have his DNA taken because he knew it wouldn't come back a match. It wouldn't come back a match because he did *not* sexually assault Michael Olsen. The semen belongs to someone else. The State has no physical evidence, so they're going to tug on your heartstrings. What happened to Michael, whoever did it, was terrible, but it wasn't Lee. His DNA was *not* a match. If it wasn't a match, that is by definition reasonable doubt. And because of that, you must find him not guilty."

Molly sat back down. Normally an opening for this type of case might take twenty minutes to an hour. She didn't want to do that, and apparently neither did Kevin. The jury had been hit with the most relevant fact: the DNA from the semen was not a match. She was hanging her entire defense on that. She didn't need to hammer it home.

The first witness was called, a detective from Sex Crimes investigating the case. His recollection of the facts in the case was detailed to the point of making the jury uncomfortable, which was good. The more uncomfortable they were, the less they were listening to what he was actually saying.

The detective went through the first encounter with Michael and the interview with Lee later. Lee had refused to speak to him and asked for a lawyer. But the detective still had to throw in that Lee appeared nervous and that in his experience, that was usually an indication of someone hiding something.

When the prosecutor was done, Molly stood up.

"Detective, you just said my client appeared nervous, correct?"

"Yes."

"Had you ever met him before that day?"

"No."

"Did you ever talk to him on the phone?"

"No."

"Did you ever hang out with him on Skype?"

"No, Counselor. We had never met prior to the events in this case."

"So you don't know my client's general level of anxiety and nervousness, do you?"

"No."

Molly leaned on the lectern with her palms. The detective wasn't being evasive. He was open and honest, which was actually worse for the defense because it was tougher to trap him. "So you can't say how he normally appears, right?"

"As far as…?"

"As far as how nervous he generally appears on any given day."

"No," the detective said, "I can't."

"Does my client have an anxiety disorder?"

"I don't know."

"Does he suffer from chronic depression?"

"I don't know."

"Does he have any mental disorder that you know about?"

"I wouldn't know about that, no."

Molly stepped around the lectern and folded her arms, staring the detective in the eyes. "Did you ask him if he had any anxiety or mental disorders?"

"No."

"So you have no idea how Lee appears or acts on any day or time except for that thirty-minute interview you had with him, correct?"

The detective hesitated, his eyes going up to the ceiling as he thought. "No, I don't know what he acts like at any other time."

"So what you saw could just be his normal level of nervousness?"

"I suppose so."

Molly went back to the lectern and leaned on it again. "Did he confess anything to you?"

"No, he did not."

"Are you aware that the semen found on Michael was tested for genetic similarity to that of my client?"

The detective was silent for a moment. "Yes."

"Was it a match?"

"As far as I'm aware, no, it was not."

"So you don't have a confession, and the semen found belonged to someone else. But you think he's guilty because he looked nervous? What kind of police work is that?"

"Objection," Kevin said, standing up.

Molly didn't want to lose momentum so she said, "Withdrawn. Detective, do you have any real evidence against my client other than the say-so of a ten-year-old boy?"

The detective was now physically uncomfortable and couldn't hide it. His face had flushed a plum color, and he was fidgeting. He wanted so badly to have her client convicted that he was upset that he was failing, and Molly knew the jury could see it.

"Cat got your tongue, Detective? I asked you if you have any evidence other than the say-so of a ten-year-old boy?"

"Those tests are wrong sometimes," he blurted out. "Your client just got lucky that it came back not a match."

Molly grinned. The officer had gone off script. "Really? How many times when a person is facing a crime have you testified that the DNA test is wrong sometimes, Detective? If I were to go back and pull your testimony from every case you've ever done—which I can do—how many times have you said it? And I remind you, you're under oath."

Kevin was on his feet again. "Your Honor, this has nothing to do with—"

"He opened the door," Molly said. "I get to go through."

The judge thought a second and said, "She's right, Mr. Renteria."

"But Your Honor, what this detective has and hasn't said in any other case—"

"If you don't want your witnesses' pasts examined, don't let them blurt things out. Go ahead, Ms. Becker."

Molly stepped close to the detective. Uncomfortably close, enough that she could smell his aftershave and wouldn't look anywhere but right into his pupils. "I asked you how many times you have testified that the DNA genetic fingerprinting test conducted by the Utah State Crime Lab is wrong."

He shook his head, looking away from the jury. "Never."

"Oh," she said, taking a few steps back and standing near the jury, "so you just happen to come out with that little tidbit now when it helps you?" Molly was on a roll. The detective looked as though he wanted to either hit her or run out of the courtroom. She decided it was worth an objection to push him. "The truth is you know these tests are accurate, but you can't stand the thought that you're wrong, can you? That you arrested an innocent man and are willing to get up there and lie to put him away so that you don't have to admit that there might be other innocent people you've put away, too."

"Up yours, Counselor."

"Enough," the judge bellowed. "Ms. Becker, you know that's crossing the line. Detective, this is my courtroom, and you will respect it while you are in that chair and not attack any officer of this court. Or I promise, I have a much more uncomfortable place for you to sit should I find you in contempt. Is that understood?"

He nodded, but didn't speak, his eyes never moving from Molly's.

Molly took a step back. She had a lot more to come at him with, but letting the jury see how badly he wanted this conviction, so badly that he was willing to lose it on the stand under routine questioning, was probably the best place to end. Besides, he wasn't the primary witness against her client. The boy was.

"No further questions," she said.

Kevin rose and asked a few questions to try to salvage his witness's testimony, but the detective had been damaged. He was stuttering now, unable to recall answers he'd already given. Kevin recognized this and hurriedly got him off the stand.

"Next witness," the judge said.

"The State calls Michael Olsen, Your Honor."

The boy shuffled through the courtroom without looking up at anyone. He was just wearing jeans and a T-shirt—what he normally would wear, Molly guessed. He took the stand, his hand shaking during the oath. His eyes were filled with fear, and for a moment, Molly wished he wasn't so young.

The fact that he was even on the stand was a victory. The State had wanted to film his testimony, as the law allowed child victims of sex crimes to record their testimony. The video would then be played for the jury. The problem was that this violated the defendant's right to cross-examine his accuser. In order for video testimony to be introduced, the judge had to view the video *in camera*, alone in his or her chambers, and determine whether cross-examination was necessary. It was, Molly thought, a joke. Cross-examination was always necessary.

At first, judges tried to protect children from testifying, but they began getting overturned on appeal. There wasn't much someone could do to hurt a judge, but having the state's Court of Appeals or the Supreme Court publicly say the judge didn't understand the law and then overturn the decision was a powerful way to get a judge to change.

Judge Veasman had been overturned twice on the issue. He now allowed defense counsel to cross-examine child victims more than six years old in person in every case.

Kevin took the lectern and waited a moment, smiling at the child. "Don't be scared, Michael. You have nothing to be scared of anymore. Okay?"

"Okay," he said softly.

"Do you remember September fifth of last year? The day we've been talking about?"

He nodded.

"You have to speak into the microphone because it's being recorded, Michael."

"Oh. Yes, I remember."

"Tell us what you remember about that day."

Michael glanced at his uncle. Kevin should have moved away from the lectern and blocked the boy's view of Lee but he hadn't, and Molly wondered if he just wasn't thinking straight or hadn't thought of it at all.

"I was at home playing *Call of Duty* and my uncle came over."

"Which uncle?"

"Uncle Lee."

"Do you see Uncle Lee here in the courtroom today?"

He nodded. "Yes."

"Where is he? Please point him out."

He lifted his hand and pointed to Lee Olsen. "That's him."

"So what did Uncle Lee do when he came over?"

The boy grew so uncomfortable that he couldn't look up, and he tried to speak but no words came out. Kevin didn't say anything. He just waited until Michael was ready and said, "Michael, please tell us what happened."

Michael looked up at his uncle and then back down at the floor. "Nothing happened."

The silence in the courtroom was so heavy that Molly heard a car passing on the road outside. She leaned back in her seat, and the chair creaked. It was like thunder rolling across the sky, and several jurors looked over at her.

"Michael," Kevin said, stepping around the lectern and

62

approaching the boy, "please tell us what happened, and be honest."

"Nothing happened. I made it up. It was someone else."

A few murmurs went up from the audience, mostly family members. Michael wasn't looking up. His gaze was glued to the floor as though he couldn't lift it. Lee Olsen wasn't looking at him either. He had his eyes on the table and the yellow legal pad Molly had given him to write notes on.

"Michael," Kevin said softly, "do you remember coming to my office several times, including yesterday? And the conversations we had?"

He nodded.

"Please speak into the microphone," the judge said.

"Yes, I remember."

"And do you remember telling me the story of how your uncle raped you?"

"Objection," Molly said, standing. "Leading."

"I need some rope, Judge," Kevin said.

"If he wants rope, there are other ways than leading the witness."

Kevin looked at her, his face contorted in anger. "Your Honor," he said sternly, "permission to treat the witness as hostile."

Surprised, Molly slowly sat down. To treat a witness as hostile meant that he thought his own witness was lying. It made it look as though he couldn't be trusted.

"Permission granted," the judge said.

"You came into my office on September ninth of last year for the first time, isn't that right?"

"Yes."

"And you'd come in then because you had just gotten out of the hospital, correct?"

"Yes."

"And you were in the hospital because your rectum—your backside, Michael—had been torn, right?"

The boy didn't answer right away. His eyes glossed over in tears. "Yes," he said softly.

"And you told me it was your Uncle Lee that did it, didn't you?"

The boy closed his eyes and tears rolled down his cheeks. Molly rose, "Your Honor, he's badgering the witness. The witness is only ten."

Kevin spun around, his eyes blazing with anger and confusion. The defense had just defended his own witness from *him* in front of the jury. His eyes locked onto Molly's, and they both knew what had happened: the case was over.

Kevin went back to the prosecution table and sat down. He had lost the jury, and everyone knew it. There was no point in him further attacking Michael.

"Any cross, Ms. Becker?" Judge Veasman asked.

"Just a few questions, Your Honor." She waited a moment, making sure the jury was paying attention to her. "Michael, did Lee Olsen inappropriately touch you in any way?"

"No."

"Was it someone else?"

He hesitated. "Yes."

"Did you lie to the police and the prosecutor?"

He nodded. "Yes."

"No further questions, Your Honor."

"Mr. Renteria, may this witness be excused?"

"Yes, Your Honor."

The judge looked between the two lawyers. "Any further witnesses, Mr. Renteria?"

Kevin stood. A forensic nurse and a child psychologist who had interviewed Michael were up next. Molly knew he could go one of two ways: he could put them on the stand and hope he could discuss why children change their testimony on the stand or not call them and rest. If he tried the former, Molly would object, stating she hadn't been given proper notice of the experts' testimony as that hadn't been what they were going to testify to. She would also argue the psychologist was not qualified to give such an assessment. She might win the objection, or she might lose; it didn't matter at this point. The prosecution's case was irreparably damaged. Nothing could save it at this point.

They did have one more option, and that was simply the jury wildcard. There was a possibility that the jury might just hate her client enough to convict, on the off chance that he had actually done it. She'd seen it happen before.

But the law was prepared for that. A directed verdict motion could be made before the jury got a chance to deliberate. The defense could say that the prosecution hadn't presented enough evidence to even go to the jury. Judge Veasman was as objective as a judge could be, and Molly knew Kevin understood that there was no way he could get past a directed verdict now.

But few prosecutors would give up this case. Kevin looked as though he wanted to fight, but he glanced back to someone in the courtroom: his boss, Vince Dale. Vince shook his head, and Kevin swallowed before saying, "The State rests, Your Honor."

"Very well. Ms. Becker?"

"Nothing from the defense."

"Alright, before I read the juror instructions and send them for deliberation, I assume the defense has a motion?"

"I do, Your Honor."

"Bailiff, clear the courtroom, please."

The bailiff, a large man with red scars on his face, rose and announced, "All rise for the jury."

Molly stood up, as did Lee Olsen. He glanced back at his wife and smiled as the jury was led out of the courtroom. When they were gone, Molly said, "At this time, the defense makes a motion for a directed verdict. The prosecution has not presented enough evidence to pass even a probable cause standard, much less beyond a reasonable doubt. They simply have not met the elements of this offense."

"Well," the judge said, "they passed probable cause at some point, since the case made it to trial."

Molly grinned. A different judge had previewed the evidence in a preliminary hearing to determine whether there was enough to prove the prosecution's case. Most prosecutors avoided giving the defense the opportunity to cross-examine the victim by submitting written statements from the victim in lieu of the victim's testimony at prelim. Here it had backfired. If Michael had come to the preliminary hearing and testified, they could've had a video of him testifying and pointing the finger at Lee to play for the jury. Instead, they had old written statements that no longer seemed relevant.

"Your Honor," Kevin began, "even with—"

"Mr. Renteria, you're not seriously going to argue that this should go to the jury, are you?"

He swallowed. "Not now, no."

The judge was silent a moment. "Okay, well, I'm granting the defense's motion and finding the State has not provided enough evidence on the elements of the case to prove to me the jury should deliberate on the matter. Your case is dismissed, Mr. Olsen. You're free to go."

Some members of Lee's family celebrated by clapping and hollering, particularly his wife and father, but not Michael. He hugged his mother, who stared with venom at Lee and led her son out of the courtroom. Lee tried to hug Molly, and she pushed him away.

"That was lucky," he said.

"Lucky my ass," she whispered. "Did you threaten that little boy?"

"What? How could you even ask me that?"

"Don't bullshit me, Lee. Did you threaten him?"

He chuckled. "You did your job and got your fucking money. Our shit is done."

Lee walked back to his family and received hugs and backslaps, then sauntered out of the courtroom as if he owned the place. Molly crossed her arms and leaned against the defense table. A couple of spectators remained, including Vince Dale. He grinned and came toward her, asking Kevin in passing, "How the hell did you not know he was going to change his testimony?"

Kevin shrugged.

"I'll deal with you later," Vince said. He turned to Molly and smiled widely as she gathered her things.

"Nice job," Vince said.

"It is what it is."

"You know he probably threatened that boy's life, right? Maybe he said he would rape his younger siblings if he didn't change his testimony."

"There's no evidence of that."

Vince chuckled and held out his arms, gesturing at the courtroom. "Since when does a courtroom have anything to do with evidence?"

Despite his abrasiveness and reputation for over-aggression—and some would say corruption—Vince and Molly had always gotten along. They were both people who had risen from nothing and made what they wanted to make of themselves. No one had given them handouts, and they molded the world around them to what they wanted it to be. They had never discussed this openly, but the understanding was there between them, unspoken and respected.

"You know, I called your office last week. You never called me back," he said.

"I know. Sorry, just busy."

"I don't think so," he said with a mischievous grin. "I think you know what I'm going to offer you, don't you?"

"I have to go, Vince. I'll talk to you later." She stopped. "Why didn't you let him finish? He had four other witnesses."

Vince shook his head. "There would be no point, and I

would've paid four other witnesses' expert fees. The first boss I ever had as a prosecutor, a drunk hillbilly from Tennessee, taught me the best philosophy a prosecutor could have: if the victim don't care, we don't care."

He smiled as she brushed past him and left the courtroom. Outside, Lee and his family were laughing and joking. She didn't see Michael anywhere near them.

10

Brigham sat in the courtroom waiting for a bailiff to arrive and unlock the back room reserved for clients to speak with their lawyers. Brigham wasn't looking forward to seeing Ted in handcuffs and a jumpsuit.

The bailiff came in and opened the door, calling Brigham's client out to see him. Ted came out into the small corridor where Brigham was standing. He'd only been in jail three days, but he looked worse, trembling and pale. It might have been Brigham's perception of him because he knew what the man was going through—the conditions he was living in, the terror from the other inmates who were all younger and stronger, the horrid meals, and the even-worse sleep that sometimes wouldn't come at all because of the fear of what his cell mate, or a guard, would do to him while he slept. Ted tried to appear brave, but to Brigham he looked like a man lost in a desert with no water in sight.

"I visited your kids," Brigham said. "They're doing okay."

"Thank you. You didn't have to do that."

Brigham nodded, glancing away. "You know, they can't be on their own. Eventually a neighbor or someone will call DCFS and they'll take them into state custody."

"Why? Monica's almost eighteen."

"Until then, they're just kids. Even when she turns eighteen, she has to show she has the ability to provide for and take care of them."

Ted thought for a moment, the look on his face fading to a deep melancholy. "Will they be together?"

"I don't know. If a foster family will take all three in. Otherwise they'll be separated."

Ted shook his head. "I can't believe I put them through this."

Brigham couldn't look him in the eyes, so he looked down at the thin file he held in his hands. Ted's file held nothing but a new-client intake sheet and a few notes. "Today's an initial appearance. We discuss bail and release, then we'll set it for a preliminary hearing."

He nodded. "Okay. Have you been paid?"

"Yes, your father called and paid with a credit card, thank you." He hesitated. "I don't think the judge is going to lower bail today, Ted. I think you'll be stuck in jail unless you can come up with fifty thousand dollars."

"I would have to use the money I set aside for my kids, and I'm not going to do that."

"If you're out, you could work. I don't know how long this case is going to take. If you're in jail, I'd have to hurry everything. I can either do a good job or a fast job, but usually not both."

He nodded. "I understand. If you think it's for the best."

"Let's have that be a last resort. First I'll see if I can convince the judge to lower the bail."

Brigham stepped back out into the courtroom. A line of attorneys filled the seats behind the defense table, ready to call their cases. Brigham stood against the wall, as there wasn't room to sit.

The cases went slowly, and Brigham did almost nothing but stare at the clock. An hour and ten minutes later, it was his turn at the lectern. "Ted Montgomery, Your Honor."

Judge Kathleen Macdow called, "Montgomery, number twelve on the calendar."

Ted was brought out and stood next to Brigham. He seemed out of place, in the wrong environment. He couldn't even stand without displaying the deep fear he was no doubt feeling.

The judge continued, "We're here for an initial appearance. Counsel?"

"Judge," Brigham said, "bail is currently set at half a million bondable. We ask that it be lowered to something more reasonable. My client has no record and deep ties to the community, including three children."

The prosecutor, who was covering initial appearances

today and someone Brigham hadn't seen before, rose. "Your Honor, he is accused of killing his wife. Frankly, I think the children are better off. And half a million on a murder case is not unreasonable. In fact, it's lower than usual."

"I would remind the court that Mr. Montgomery hasn't been convicted of anything yet," Brigham said halfheartedly. The truth was, the State didn't need a conviction. Accusing people was enough to ruin their lives, and even judges assumed guilt during the bail phase. "Also," Brigham continued, "the allegation is that Mr. Montgomery's wife was dying of incurable cancer, and this was a mercy killing. My client is not a danger to anyone in the community."

"I'm keeping bail where it is," the judge replied. "Preliminary hearing before Judge Lawrence on… April fourteenth at two."

"That works," Brigham said. "If I may be excused, Your Honor."

"You may, thank you."

Brigham turned to Ted. "I'll call your father and see what we can do."

Ted nodded, scanning the audience, probably for his children. The bailiff grabbed his arm roughly and said, "Eyes forward."

"Hey," Brigham said, "take it easy."

The bailiff gave him a stern look and yanked Ted away.

74

Confronting the bailiff had been a rookie mistake. They couldn't do anything to the attorneys, so the bailiff would take out his aggression on Ted.

Brigham left the courtroom and headed for the elevators. He stopped in front and checked his phone. Several potential clients had called, and the discovery on Ted Montgomery was in his inbox.

11

The courthouse was too loud. It was shaped like a dome, and everything echoed, including the people shouting bids at the real estate auctions in a corner on the bottom floor. Brigham went outside and sat on the steps facing State Street, where he opened and read Ted's file.

It held nothing surprising. His wife, Ruby, had been suffering from cancer for more than a year. Her nurse and several doctors had been interviewed, and Ted had asked all of them if there was anything they could do to alleviate her pain. One of the oncologists had told the police that Ted had asked him point-blank to end his wife's pain. When he refused, Ted told him it was cruel of him to deny her.

Brigham's biggest question was where the morphine had come from, and the police had been unable to answer it other than guessing that it had likely come from the hospital pharmacy. He didn't know much about how hospital pharmacies dispensed medications, particularly opiates, but he guessed getting them wasn't as simple as just asking for them. Prescriptions were probably forged, although there was no record of it. He made a note to find out where the morphine had come from and how Ted got hold of it.

Unfortunately, Ted had given a full confession, which had been recorded. Brigham would have to get that later. But the detective's summation pretty much covered it all: Ted had gone through every detail of how he'd hooked up the morphine to her drip and how he'd brought his kids up to spend time with their mother as she died. He said several times that it was peaceful and that she had finally found some comfort. It was clear Ted didn't feel he'd done anything wrong.

Brigham's guts were tied in knots, and he had to take several deep breaths to relax himself. Reading the details of the morphine and how Ruby had closed her eyes and how her breathing had slowed dredged up something he hadn't thought about in a long time. It threw him off, and he didn't like that.

He checked the time on his phone. He had to be in West Jordan for a hearing on a shoplifting case. He retrieved his bike and headed for the train.

By six in the evening, court was finished, and all the potential-client calls had been returned. More paperwork still needed to be completed and more motions drafted, but Brigham didn't feel like doing that right now. Right now, he needed a drink.

The Oatmeal Pub near his apartment was rarely occupied

by more than a few people at a time. They served little more than beer but had more than two hundred varieties. Brigham ordered the first one that looked appealing, a brown sugar oatmeal stout, and drank by himself at the bar.

The dark amber fluid swirled with bubbles, and he watched the froth as it bubbled over the mug and onto the slick bar. The sheer number of bars in Salt Lake had been a surprise to him when he'd moved here from Louisiana. Utah was seen as being dominated by the temperate Mormon faith, but he'd found downtown Salt Lake had more bars per mile than anywhere near his law school of Tulane in New Orleans.

He pushed the mug away when it was still half full. As it turned out, the beer wasn't what he had come here for. The solitude was what he had needed. For so long, he had fought to get where he was: a partner in his own law firm, in demand, and in court every day. Now that he had it, it seemed like nothing but more effort.

The work was enjoyable for the most part. The majority of his clients were normal, everyday people who had made mistakes. There were some gangsters and sex offenders of course, who couldn't or wouldn't change for anything, but by and large his clients were decent people who had done bad things. The surprise was how many of them came back to him. Even within a year, he was seeing the same names over and over again. People who just couldn't change their behavior to follow the laws. The question was what to do with them, and he didn't have an answer.

"Scotty said you'd be here."

Rebecca sat down next to him. She pushed up her glasses and put both hands on the bar, glancing over the bottles of beer set up in front of a mirror.

"It's quiet, and nobody really comes here."

"*Nobody* as in lawyers and judges, you mean?"

He nodded, playing with the coaster his mug sat on. "I don't like talking about law all the time. I need time away from it."

"Well, you're not gonna like this, then: a reporter from Channel 2 wants to interview you about Ted Montgomery."

"No. Definitely not. Tell them 'no comment' for right now."

"Can I ask you something? It seemed like you didn't want to take that case. Every defense attorney in town is jealous, according to Scotty. You should be psyched."

He shook his head. "I'm not."

"Why?"

Brigham rose and laid a five on the bar. "How was your first day?"

She grinned. "That sensitive, huh?"

"Something I'd rather not talk about. But on the subject of Ted, I'd like you to do the case with me."

"Really? I'm, like, brand new."

"Doesn't matter. I always interview the jury after a verdict. Two separate cases we won, both Scotty's cases that he did with me, the jurors said they were impressed that we had two lawyers on the case. So now I try to have two attorneys at the table on the major cases."

"Well, I'm flattered to be a prop already."

He grinned. "Just be at the office early so we can watch the interviews."

As he was walking out, he heard Rebecca order a mixed drink. The men in the bar were eyeing her, but she didn't seem to notice. He turned and left. The DA's office should've been nearly empty by now.

12

The Salt Lake County District Attorney's Office took up several floors of a skyscraper in the heart of downtown. Numerous law firms, accounting firms, and investment companies shared the building, and it had the air of being expensive office space rather than a government building.

Brigham rode up to the fifth floor. The receptionist was still there, but most of the staff, he knew, checked out at five p.m.

"Hello," she said behind bulletproof glass. "Who are you here to see?"

"Whoever is handling Ted Montgomery. Homicide at the Matheson. I'm the defense attorney on it."

"Hm," she said, checking her computer. "Looks like that's Debra Flynn. I'll buzz her."

She pressed a button on her phone, and Brigham went to look out floor-to-ceiling windows with a view of the gym across the street and the investment bank across from that. Cops, prosecutors, defense attorneys, and witnesses were still coming in and out of the building even though the office was closed, for all intents and purposes. The county's DA office filed more cases every year than the rest of the DA's offices in the state combined. Though Salt Lake was a medium-sized city, the crime rate was growing to that of a large city.

"She'll see you now," the receptionist said. "I just need your Bar card."

Brigham handed it over and was buzzed into the offices. The receptionist led him to an office tucked away in a corridor with a painting of Salt Lake fifty years ago hanging in it.

A woman he had seen in court several times but had never spoken with sat at a large desk, a wall of glass behind her with a view of the setting sun.

"Thank you," he said to the receptionist as he stepped inside the office.

He didn't see any dust anywhere in the office, no decorations on the walls, and the law books on the shelves were glistening. The windows were spotless, even more so than those in the lobby, and the desk shone, buffed to a high polish. The room smelled of lemons.

"Please sit," she said, not looking up from her computer.

Brigham sat and waited quietly as she finished typing what looked like an email. When she was through, she closed her browser and leaned back in the chair. A slight smile parted her lips, and Brigham smiled back.

"You're Brigham?"

"Yeah."

"I think you're the only person that's made Vince wig out. He's usually very calm. When he lost that murder trial against you last year, he came back to the office and started throwing things at people."

"That sounds about right."

She shrugged. "People love him or hate him, same as anyone else. I happen to like him. He's direct. That's hard to find. Most people will lie to you, even about stuff they don't need to lie about. Vince never does that."

He nodded, glancing at a photo on her desk. It appeared to be her and someone who looked like Dick Cheney, but Brigham couldn't tell.

"So," she said, "you're here for Ted Montgomery. Let's hear your sales pitch."

"No pitch. I just want to know what your thoughts are about it."

She shrugged. "My thoughts are that he killed his wife in front of his children."

"Those are the facts. But what are your *thoughts* about it?"

She leaned forward. "I think I'd like to give him the death penalty, but our capital punishment team turned the case down. So I'll have to settle for fifteen to life."

"That's it?"

"That's it."

"It doesn't matter that she was in extreme pain and begged

him every day to end her life?"

She shook her head, a mocking grin on her face. "You're not allowed to murder people because you think they ask for it. What if she would've changed her mind the next day?"

Brigham hesitated. "I know where you're coming from. I understand it. But those kids don't have anyone else. They'll be put in state custody without him."

"I think that's for the best. What if he believes one of them is asking for it?"

Brigham was about to say something rude but held his tongue. Instead he said, "So you have no offer?"

"Three to life. I'll lower it to attempted homicide as a legal fiction."

Brigham shook his head. She thought he was inexperienced enough not to know that wasn't any kind of deal. "The parole board will keep him for twenty years. I've taken all five members of the board to lunch and gotten their views of different cases."

She smiled. "Then you're one of the smart ones. But that's my offer. And it expires at prelim."

Brigham nodded and rose. "I'll take it to him. Nice meeting you."

"You as well." As Brigham turned to leave, she said, "Hey, how's that client of yours? Amanda something, the one that got away from Vince? He's hoping she'll screw up so he gets a second shot."

"She had a nervous breakdown and was institutionalized at UNI for a few weeks. The last time I visited her, she was doing better. She's even got a job and is going to church again. Tell Vince he's not going to get his second shot."

Brigham left. Despite his calm demeanor, anger bubbled in his gut. The arrogance was too much. Some of the DA's people felt they were above everyone else, that somehow their actions were more pure than those of the people they prosecuted. Brigham felt anyone anywhere could be right where his client was.

A phrase went through his mind: "There but for the grace of God go I."

He hadn't understood it as a kid, but he understood it now.

13

The night fell over Salt Lake City quickly, revealing a full moon. Brigham was back in his office, staring at the moon through his windows, when Scotty shuffled in. The man sat across from him, twitched his eyelids a few times, and said, "What's the matter?"

He shook his head. "Some cases get to me. Some *people* get to me."

"Any people in particular?"

"Do you remember that client we had, Melanie… what was her last name? Robbins or Robinson or something?"

"Tall, blonde… Don't remember her case, though."

"Heroin possession. She had a long history, so they wanted to lock her up. When she was ten years old, she'd run away from home because her stepfather was raping her. She turned to prostitution to survive until her twenties, when she cleaned up her act. She'd had a relapse and got busted with the heroin. The prosecutor, this joker who went to Harvard, told me that if she didn't want to go to jail, she shouldn't break the law. Like it was that easy. And I just thought, let's see you go through what she went through and see how you turn out. That asshole was just clueless, but the state gave him the power to judge people worthy and unworthy of mercy."

Scotty looked down at his shoes. "That's how it's always been. And be grateful. Some countries just have people stamping files 'guilty' and 'not guilty.' No jury or judge to look it over, no one to hear the evidence. We're lucky with what we have. With human nature."

"Human nature?"

"Most people don't think. They just act. I think it'll lead to our destruction as a species." He loosened his tie. "My first wife used to tell me that. Or maybe I would tell her? I can't remember. We were both drunk through the marriage."

"I don't buy that prediction. People are good, Scotty. Or at least they want to be. I think they just don't know how."

He shrugged. "Maybe." He rose and headed for the door. "Not from what I've seen, though."

Brigham called it a night somewhere around nine p.m. after going through the discovery in Ted's case again. The State, from what he could tell, was going to call at least three witnesses: the detective who got the confession, the treating oncologist who denied Ted's request to terminate Ruby's life, and the nurse who was taking care of Ruby during the day. No one else was terribly relevant, though the State would probably call the medical examiner to discuss cause of death. In cases like this, the defense sometimes simply agreed on the cause of death, and they skipped the ME. Brigham decided to do that. No one had any doubt how Ruby died, and calling the ME to the stand to discuss morphine overdoses and show autopsy photos wouldn't win any points with the jury.

Besides, the ME alone would take an entire day of testimony, and juries got impatient and wanted to hurry things along and get out of there. Research showed that with each additional day a trial lasted, jurors spent two hours less per day paying attention. After two days, their attention spans covered the first four hours of court and dwindled exponentially from there. He guessed this would be a three- or four-day trial. That meant the jurors, by day three, would be able to pay attention to only two hours of testimony in an entire day.

Brigham got on his bike and rode casually on the sidewalk, not rushing anywhere. The Trax train had bike racks, and he stopped and got on the train heading south, away from his apartment. He sat near the window and stared out over the city. The image of his grandfather kept coming back to him, and he pushed it out of his mind.

It had started to storm, and the rain spattered against the windows of Trax. Since Katrina, storms gave him an uneasy feeling. Something like sensing danger when walking down the street when no danger was really there.

When Hurricane Katrina had torn apart New Orleans, it'd felt like the end of the world. Brigham had lived twenty miles outside of town and was spared most of nature's brutality, but when things had settled, he went back and saw the utter destruction nature could cause, as if it decided to show humanity that they weren't the top dogs on the planet. That was a lesson that was hard to forget.

The train looped around and headed back downtown. The moon shone brightly through thin clouds as if swimming in a blue-black soup. Brigham watched it through the window as people entered and exited the train. When he was back downtown, he retrieved his bike, got off, and headed to Molly's through the rain.

Molly lived in an upscale condo complex in the city. She'd bought it when she was making the most money in her life, as a drone associate at a large firm. She'd left when she realized she was miserable and didn't want to be one of the partners who were drunk every day after work and sobered up on their way to work the next morning.

The security guard buzzed Brigham in but made him leave his bike in the lobby. He went to her floor and knocked on the door. She answered wearing jeans and a sweatshirt, a glass of wine in her hand. He stepped inside without a word and kissed her on the cheek.

Brigham crossed the living room and collapsed on the

couch, catching a glimpse of the moon again through her living room windows. He leaned back and didn't speak as Molly sat next to him and set her wine on the coffee table. She began massaging his left elbow. He'd fractured it once on a motorcycle, riding at over a hundred miles an hour on a dare. It ached at random times, and Molly knew when it was because she said his face would bunch up like a bulldog's.

"Have I told you congrats on your win?" Brigham asked.

"No."

He looked at her and she wouldn't meet his eyes. "Why do I get the impression you're not super proud?"

She reached for her wine with one hand, her other still rubbing his elbow. "I think he intimidated the victim. Do I have a duty to report something like that?"

"You can't if it's just a suspicion. You need evidence, and even then you're going against the interests of your client. You could be disbarred. We're mercenaries who don't betray their employers. Scotty says we're samurai with shitty masters."

She chuckled. "He does have a way with words."

He looked up into her eyes. "You can't control what they do. You can only advise them, fight for them, and the rest is out of your hands. They're adults."

She shook her head. "That poor kid. As if he hadn't been through enough. And his father is even worse—he told me he thought it should be handled within the family, and the government has no reason to get involved. Their idea of punishment was not letting the uncle near their kids anymore. But even that will probably fade over time."

"The world's a mess. It's always going to be a mess. Just try to straighten out your little corner of it."

"What, are you reading a book of quotes or something?"

"I may have watched a Buddha documentary on PBS recently."

She ran her fingers over his forehead, grinning. "I love the way your eyes reflect the moonlight. They change color. I know it's just an illusion, but I like that idea, that we change based on how the universe perceives us." She exhaled loudly and looked out the windows. "I think I'd like to take tomorrow off and go somewhere. Down to Moab and go hiking or something."

"I have four appearances in the morning. But I can take off after."

"It's a date then."

"Yup."

She leaned down and softly pressed her lips to his.

14

In the morning, Brigham woke and kissed Molly before leaving. The hot morning sun warmed him on the bike ride back to his apartment and dried out the city from the previous night's rain. He showered, changed into a suit, thought about how his accountant had told him none of his suits fit properly, and then left.

All of his hearings were in the South Salt Lake Justice Court, all DUIs. That seemed to be one of two offenses not bound by any socioeconomic status: both rich and poor got DUIs and sex offenses in equal numbers.

The prosecutor was a young woman with red hair who wore her skirt just a little too high. She was flirtatious with the male defense attorneys and standoffish with the female ones. Brigham waited for his turn to speak to her, staring at the odd blue carpet of the courtroom. The place looked like a large office that had been hastily converted to a court.

"Hey, Janine," Brigham said.

"Brigham, how are ya?"

"Not bad," he said, sitting down next to her at the

prosecution table. "How's Mark?"

"He might be transferring jobs soon."

"The wedding's next year, isn't it?"

"Yeah, but we might rush that. All our family is here and he might be transferring to Montana. We'd have to come back for the wedding."

"Well, don't forget my invite."

"I won't." She flipped through her stack of files and pulled out a pack of four held together by a rubber band. "Impaired driving on all four?"

"We did have an issue on that one," he said, pointing to one of the files. "The officer on that didn't have his certification on the Intox. Not a huge deal, but I think it warrants a reckless driving."

"Just 'cause his certs were expired?"

"He's a specialist in DUI arrests, and he let his DUI certifications expire. I'm sure there's more there if I dig. But the reckless makes us go away."

She grunted playfully. "Fine. But don't tell anyone else I gave you that."

"I won't."

The four cases were pleaded out. Forms were filled out, and each client was assigned alcohol classes and fines. The fines were, of course, what the courts cared most about. Fines were on the high side in that court, but it was nearly impossible to

93

get the judge to impose jail time on this offense, so it was a good trade-off.

Brigham was out of the courtroom by ten. The sun was still bright in the sky, and the clouds that had hung over the city for the past few days were gone. Brigham rode back to work to check in. Molly was in her office, staring off into space, a pen lightly touching her lips.

"Lost in thought?" he said.

"Hm? No, I'm fine. You ready to leave?"

"Yeah, just wanted to close out a couple of things for tomorrow. We'll be back Monday, though, right?"

"If we have to be," she said with a sigh.

"We'll play it by ear."

Her phone rang, and she looked at it, a little puzzled.

"Who is it?" Brigham asked.

"Vince Dale." She answered. "Vince… yeah… yeah, but… now? Right now? Okay, as a favor to you. Bye."

"What's up?"

"He says he needs to show me something."

"Show you what?"

"He said I need to see it rather than hear it. He's coming by to pick me up."

Brigham thought for a moment. "I should go with you."

"I'm fine, Brigham."

"I don't trust him."

"I've known the guy ten years. He's not that bad. Most people just misunderstand him."

Brigham leaned against her doorframe. "There's nothing to misunderstand. He craves power. That's what this is all about for him. It has nothing to do with serving the public. It's just power."

"Maybe. But maybe, growing up in an abusive, poor home where you have no power will do that to you."

"I don't buy his whole pulling-himself-up-by-the-bootstraps thing."

She rose and stretched her arms. "I'll be back in half an hour. Unless we decide to make out for a while."

"Not funny."

She tapped his chest on the way out. He turned and walked to his office, crumpling into his chair before opening a file on his desk about a pot charge. He put his feet up and began reading.

Molly waited outside in the sunshine. Sometimes she felt like a cave dweller. Once, she'd added up all the hours she spent indoors on a single day: twenty-three. Twenty-three out of twenty-four hours were spent indoors, and the only hour she was outside was walking to and from places. She pictured her ancestors foraging for food on the Serengeti, easily getting ten or more hours of sunshine a day, and wondered if all the problems of the world were caused by people just not getting outside enough.

Vince rolled to a stop in front of her in his black BMW. She climbed into the passenger seat, and he grinned as he pulled away.

"You're the most beautiful woman I've had in here. Maybe I should drive us around a little and make everyone else jealous."

"Maybe you'd like me to file a lawsuit against the county. I'm sure they'd appreciate a million-dollar harassment suit in your first year as DA."

He smiled. "It'd be worth it."

"So, what do you need to show me?"

"It's up here."

They drove up State Street and turned right into a neighborhood of run-down buildings and neglected streets and sidewalks. Billboards advertised products or services she'd never heard of, like Mexican sodas and all-Vietnamese accounting firms.

They stopped in front of a modest home with a chain-link fence around it. Two police cruisers were parked in front, as well as an ambulance and a fire truck.

"What is this?" she asked.

"This," he said, glaring at the house, "is the home of Erik

Olsen. Lee Olsen's brother, and the father of Michael Olsen."

The paramedics were standing on the sidewalk talking to each other when a black van pulled up from the medical examiner's office.

"What happened?" she asked, her heart beating faster. There were two things that might've happened, but as Vince had brought her all the way down here, she knew which one it was.

"Michael Olsen, only ten years old, shot himself with his father's gun. His mother found him. He went to the garage and did it there. No note. I don't think he realized that you're supposed to leave a note when you kill yourself."

Molly's stomach churned, and the bile rising in her chest and throat felt as though it might spew out despite her control. "Why did you bring me here?" she asked quietly.

"Because I wanted you to see the full repercussions of your work. Sometimes prosecutors and defense attorneys are detached from all the consequences."

"You want to shame me. Well, you can't. We're not the Soviet Union."

"Oh, give me some credit. I wouldn't want to live in a society that doesn't have defense attorneys. I'm just saying that some people are cut out for prosecution, and some people are cut out for defense. You're not a defense attorney. You never have been."

One of the paramedics spoke with the medical examiner's people, and they all went inside. Michael's mother was weeping on the front porch, a police officer sitting next to her speaking quietly. She looked away. She didn't want to see a gurney with a small body on it being taken out of the house.

"I'd like to go now."

"Sure."

He pulled away. She kept her eyes on the road ahead of them. The neighborhood grew more decrepit. She saw a car taken apart completely, the pieces strewn on the lawn like decorations. Children were playing on the engine block as if it were a playground.

"I can't believe you showed me that," she said.

"You would've found out eventually."

"You did it just to get what you want. Brigham was right about you."

He smiled. "And what did Boy Wonder say about me?"

"He said all you care about is power."

"He's more perceptive than I thought. I do care about power. But it's power for a greater good. There's a wave of evil just out under the surface of society, Molly. It's under us, around us. It's closing in and growing more frightening every second. It doesn't care about wealth or if you're a good person or if you stay out of trouble or not. It affects everybody. And the only line of defense we have is our cops and prosecutors.

We're holding it back. But without good people, the wave will crash through us. What I do, I do for the greater good. I do it so mothers will feel comfortable letting their kids play outside and so people don't have to carry guns everywhere they go because they're scared they're gonna get shot or robbed. I want the world to be a better place, and I'm making that happen the only way I know how."

He pulled the car over to the side of the road. She couldn't look at him. She kept her eyes on a fire hydrant and the way the sun shining down through the trees speckled it gold.

"Are you ready to hear my offer now? Or do you want to wait until the next Michael Olsen?"

Molly swallowed. "No," she said softly. "I'll hear it."

15

Brigham stood outside the courtroom, waiting in line at the metal detectors. Sometimes the lines were short, usually when he wasn't running late. Other times it took half an hour just to get through the detectors and onto the elevators.

In the past month, he had investigated every part of the Montgomery case. He'd interviewed everyone at the hospital, every officer who'd had anything to do with the case, and had gone through everything with Ted. He felt prepared, though once he got people on the stand, he was never really sure what they were going to say.

A woman in a tight skirt was giving the bailiffs trouble because they were insisting she take her heels off, as they were setting off the detectors. She was arguing, waving her hands wildly. Brigham had seen it before. The bailiff dealing with her, a man with scars on the left side of his face, was the least patient of them. He frequently badgered people and was even rumored to have once punched a drunk trying to get through. Brigham thought he would have been fired if that were true, but then again cops stuck together, and when one was in trouble, they tended to back each other up.

The woman was pulled aside and handcuffed. Most of the people in line breathed a sigh of relief. She sat in a chair and yelled a little more, then gave up and stared down at the floor. When Brigham got through the metal detectors and wanding, he took out one of his business cards and slipped it into her jacket pocket.

"Call me after they write your ticket. It'll be for disorderly conduct. I'll take care of it for free."

"Thanks," she said. "I don't want to take my heels off. I have a prosthetic. I tried to tell them I didn't want to take it off."

"It's okay. Just call me," he said, hurrying to the elevators.

When he stepped out onto his floor, he received a text from Molly. *Need to have lunch with you today.*

In Ted Montgomery's prelim right now. Don't know if I can make lunch

Dinner?

Sure

The courtroom was packed with press. Some judges allowed cameras and others didn't. Judge Lawrence, a slim woman who liked to drink a Big Gulp while on the bench, allowed them. Brigham guessed she liked seeing herself on the news.

At the prosecution table, the lead detective on Ted's case, Henry Sean, sat with Debra Flynn. The detective was wearing a shirt and tie, but the tattoos that covered his arms poked out of his shirtsleeves. He looked at Brigham and then away again.

Brigham sat down and put his satchel on the table. This was when most of the plea bargaining in criminal cases really happened. He swiveled his chair around to face Debra, and she did the same.

"Manslaughter as a second," he said. "One to fifteen."

"No way. If it weren't in front of his kids, maybe."

"He wanted them to say goodbye to her."

"He wanted to be selfish and scarred them for the rest of their lives."

"Debra, this guy is well respected and doesn't have a traffic ticket on his record. It isn't worth the waste of money it'd be to stick him in prison for the rest of his life."

"Maybe you can get the board to sympathize with him and let him out after the minimum."

He shook his head. There was only one person on the Board of Pardons that Brigham considered softhearted enough to recommend early release for someone convicted of a homicide. A former social worker. But he was the least vocal member, and the other four, from what he'd heard, routinely bullied him out of positions. The other four were prior prosecutors, cops or defense attorneys. All careers that tended to leave people jaded.

"Attempted homicide as a second."

"No, I'm not giving him anything that gets him one to fifteen. I want life as my upper boundary."

"Why? He's, like, fifty. You want him to die in prison?"

She opened her mouth to speak, but then her face contorted a moment. The two of them held each other's gaze.

"Seriously?" Brigham said. "You *want* him to die in prison?"

"I never said that."

"You didn't have to. Look, if that's your stance, just be up front with me right now so we don't waste months trying to plead him to something. For the sake of your future self and mine, just be honest with me."

She shrugged. "I don't like what he did or how he did it. That woman may have wanted to live the next day."

Brigham leaned back in his seat and stared at the judge's empty bench. Nothing he could say was going to persuade her. Many times, if plea bargaining had failed before prelim, he was able to work something out right before a trial. But he was usually more aggressive than that. He'd call the prosecutor and harass them until they had a deal in place or show up at their office. Somehow, he knew that wouldn't work with her. He had to find another way.

"All rise," the bailiff called. "Third District Court is now in session. The Honorable Kameron J. Lawrence presiding."

"Be seated," the judge said as she flipped open her

computer. "Any summary matters?"

Three other attorneys had settled their cases, so they stood at the lectern one by one, waived their preliminary hearings, and asked for the cases to be set before the assigned judge. The preliminary hearing judge was different from the assigned judge, so she couldn't take pleas. This was a safety precaution, since preliminary hearing judges heard most of the evidence, and it could affect them during trial. But it was a practice Brigham had seen only in the Third District. Everywhere else in Utah, it was the same judge, and forget objectivity.

"All right," the judge said after the pleas. "How are we looking on the Montgomery matter?"

Debra stood up. "The State is ready to proceed in that matter, Your Honor."

Brigham rose. He'd been so shocked by Debra's stance that his client should die in prison that he'd forgotten to check the courtroom for Ted. He turned around and scanned the room. Of the twenty or so people there, none of them were Ted. He had bailed out a while ago and should have been there. "The defense will be ready as soon as my client gets here."

"He's twenty minutes late, Mr. Theodore."

"Just ten more minutes, Your Honor. I'm sure he'll be here."

"Okay, court is in recess for ten minutes. Please have the bailiffs notify me when your client shows up."

104

"All rise," the bailiff said as the judge left.

Brigham went over to the bailiff. "Do you have Ted in custody?"

The bailiff scanned a sheet in front of him. "No, I'm showing he bailed out two weeks ago."

Brigham scanned the audience again. Then he hurried out of the courtroom and looked down both sides of the hallway. It was possible Ted was in the wrong courtroom. They were in front of a different judge from last time, and he could just be sitting in the other courtroom.

He took the elevators one floor higher and stepped off into a crowd of people trying to get on. He pushed his way through and jogged down the long corridor until he came to Judge Macdow's courtroom. The doors were locked: court wasn't in session. He searched the rest of the hallways and then went back to his floor and searched. Ted wasn't there.

Brigham went back to the courtroom and got Ted's file. He dialed the cell number they had for him, and it went to voicemail.

"Ted, this is your lawyer. You're supposed to be in court right now. Please call me back."

As he was slipping the phone into his pocket, he caught a glimpse of Debra staring at him.

"You seem amused," he said.

"I told you. He knows what he did. He's gone."

105

"No way. Why would he hire me and then take off?"

"He hired you because he knew he was more likely to be released with an attorney. Probably to have you try to lower the bail, too."

Brigham shook his head. He had a sense for when clients were going to run. One of his was from a wealthy family from Mexico, and he was charged with aggravated robbery, looking at fourteen to life. Brigham knew he would run at some point. But Ted… no way. She was wrong.

"I think he forgot or something happened. Car trouble or something."

"Yeah," she scoffed. "Car trouble."

The ten minutes turned to twenty before the judge came out. Brigham had spent the entire time trying Ted's cell phone, calling the office to ask if he'd come by there, and calling the emergency contact they had listed for him—a brother in Oregon, who never picked up.

"Well?" the judge asked.

"Your Honor, I don't know where my client is."

She nodded. "What's the State's position? I'm inclined to issue a warrant."

"I would ask for a no-bail warrant, Your Honor."

"Your Honor, we have no idea what happened. He could

be in the hospital right now because he was in an accident."

Debra said, "Then let's hope no one decides to put him out of his misery."

This drew a few chuckles. Brigham didn't find it funny. "Judge, give me twenty-four hours. If I can't find him, issue the warrant then."

"A reasonable request. You've got twenty-four hours to get him before me. The warrant issues automatically at ten tomorrow morning. Anything else?"

"No, Your Honor," Debra said.

"No, Your Honor. And thank you."

"Court is adjourned. Thank you both."

16

Brigham hurried back to the office. He checked with his paralegals, hoping he'd received a message from Ted while he was out, but no message was waiting for him. Scotty hadn't heard from him either.

He ran to Molly's office and said, "You haven't heard from Ted Montgomery, have you?"

"No. Why?"

"He wasn't in court. He's got twenty-four hours to make an appearance or a warrant issues."

"Huh. Well, maybe he's on a beach in Mexico somewhere?"

"He paid us a bunch of money. He wouldn't have done that if he knew he wasn't going to fight the case. I think something happened."

Molly hesitated. "I need to talk to you, Brigham. I've been thinking about something the past few weeks. It's important."

"Can it wait? I've lost a client."

She nodded. "Sure. Dinner then?"

"Yeah, dinner."

He dashed to his office and called his private investigator.

Private investigators were a defense attorney's right hand. The prosecutors had the police department, and defense attorneys had their investigators, who were usually just former cops anyway.

Brigham had found the perfect investigator for his particular style: Jennifer Vest, a former homicide detective with a master's in criminal justice. She answered on the second ring.

"Hey, Brigham," she said. "I was just thinking about you, actually."

"I would normally be flattered, but I'm in a little bit of a rush, Jen."

"I was curious what happened with that Mendoza case we had."

"Settled with a misdemeanor and no jail."

"That's great. That's what you guys were shooting for. So what's up?"

"I have a client who didn't show up to court, and I need to find him in the next twenty-four hours."

"All right. What's his name?"

"Ted Montgomery."

"The guy in the news?"

"That's him. I'm going to transfer you to Lexi, and she'll give you all the information we have. I'm afraid he may have fled the country."

"I'll do my best. No guarantees."

"None needed. Thanks. Oh, actually, I did have one more thing. Lower priority, so do it later."

"Okay, shoot."

"I have a client named Jessica Padilla charged with a DUI in Salt Lake City. The chief prosecutor, Gwen Henries, won't allow any deals on it. She never gets involved with deals unless there's media attention. I think there's some other connection between the two, but Jessica says she's never met her."

"Gotcha. Okay, I'll hurry with the Montgomery thing."

"Thanks. And if he is fleeing the country, I don't want TSA alerted because of us."

"Understood. I should have something soon."

"Thanks again."

Brigham hung up and then paced his office for a few minutes. He wasn't sure what else to do right now. He'd blocked himself out on the office calendar so he could just work on the Montgomery case today, and now that he had the time, he wished he had something to occupy him.

Scotty came into the office and sat down without being asked. "I lose clients all the time."

"I know. I kinda hope he took off. But his kids—"

Brigham froze. Then he dashed out of the office without explanation.

By the time Brigham arrived at the Montgomery home, it was well past lunch, and he'd skipped breakfast. His stomach was growling, but he pushed the thought of food out of his mind and ran up to the porch. He knocked and waited. Then he rang the doorbell and knocked again. No answer. He realized he didn't even know what the children did during the day. He guessed they were all in school and felt foolish that he'd run all the way down here. He'd have to try to find out where the local schools were and see if the children were there. If they weren't, he had no doubt that Ted was gone.

As he was stepping off the porch, he glanced back through the window. He could see all the way through the living room into the kitchen and the back door. Light came through. He turned around and glared through the window. The back door was open.

Brigham raced around the house, hoping one of the neighbors wouldn't mistakenly shoot him as a prowler. The back door was wide open, probably from the wind, which was pushing it against the wall periodically.

He stepped into the house. The kitchen appeared about the same. As he went through to the living room, something was different, but he couldn't tell what. He scanned from one side of the room to the other.

A noise startled him. A crash—something falling and hitting a bare floor. Brigham's heart raced, and he turned in the direction of the noise, somewhere deeper in the house.

"Hello?" he said. "Anyone home?"

Taking a few steps into the corridor linking the living room with the rest of the house, he paused and listened. He could hear wind chimes outside and some children yelling up the street. The sunshine was pouring through the windows, and he watched the swirling dust in the beams. Farther down the hallway, past what he guessed was a bathroom and a bedroom, was a set of stairs leading down. He walked cautiously down the hallway and stopped at the top of the stairs.

It was dark down in the basement, no lights on. The stairs took a sharp left about six steps down, and he couldn't see what was around that corner. The thought of three kids here by themselves wasn't comforting, and his immediate thought was that someone had broken in. He didn't carry a gun, so he searched for a weapon. In one of the boys' rooms was an aluminum baseball bat. He grabbed it and headed down the stairs.

After every step, he paused and listened. No more noises came, and he wondered if he'd just heard something random in the house. But it had sounded like pots or something else made of metal falling onto cement.

He took the corner, ready to swing with the bat if someone rushed him. A few more steps, and he was on the basement level. He found the light switch and flipped it on.

The basement was unfinished. The floors were bare cement, and dangling lightbulbs lit the space. Rows of steel shelves were lined with tools and boxes.

In the center of the room was a pile of tools: screwdrivers, wrenches, hammers, pliers. It looked as though it'd fallen from a shelf that was oddly placed about five feet from the nearest wall and in the most inconvenient location if anyone tried to walk through.

Brigham approached the tools in the center of the floor. His eyes darted around the room, his fingers clenched around the bat. He stared at every dark corner until he was certain there was nothing there.

When he got to the tools, he bent down and went through them. Nothing interesting there. He rose and caught sight of a door on the far end of the basement that led to the next room. It was open about six inches.

Holding the bat up, he tiptoed over to the door and peeked inside. Bent over a large box was a man in jeans and a flannel shirt. Brigham, his heart pounding so loudly it seemed to drown out any other sound, slowly pushed the door open wider and tightened his grip on the bat.

"Who are you?"

The man jumped as if he'd been shocked with a cattle prod. The papers in his hands went flying around the room, a look of utter terror on his face.

"Who are you?" Brigham shouted.

"Who the hell are you?"

"What are you doing in Ted's house?"

"I'm his brother. Who the hell are you?"

Brigham, now that he heard it, could see it. The man was pudgier with less hair, but he could see it. "You're his brother?"

"Yeah, Timothy. I'm down here from Portland, man."

"I'm his lawyer, Brigham."

The fear in the man's eyes seemed to fade. "Do all lawyers carry bats into people's houses?"

"I came to check on his kids. I thought someone had broken in."

"No, man. I got the kids. They're with my wife at a restaurant."

Brigham lowered the bat. "Sorry," he said. He leaned the bat against the wall. "What're you doing here?"

"We came to watch the kids. Ted called and said he needed us to come down for a few weeks until his trial."

"Do you know where he is?"

"Yeah, he's with the kids."

"I need you to take me to him."

17

Most of the day was spent on paperwork. Every time a defense attorney filed a motion, Debra had the option of responding or not. The Utah Rules of Criminal Procedure allowed her to skip responding to a motion until after the hearing if she wanted. Most prosecutors saved themselves the trouble and didn't respond right away. Prosecutors won about 95 percent of all motions filed anyway.

But Debra couldn't do that. A motion to her was a challenge: an attorney had said her case was flawed. She felt it was almost a personal attack. Every motion filed on any of her cases was responded to. And unlike the prosecutors in her division, she didn't have some law student intern write her motion responses. She wrote every single one and argued them herself when they had the hearing.

The motion she had just finished was simple but effective. The defense attorney had challenged probable cause to arrest, stating that the real reason the defendant was arrested was because he was Mexican, and the officer assumed he was illegal. Once he was under arrest, Immigration and Customs Enforcement could put a hold on him, meaning he would not get out of jail no matter what. Once the criminal case was completed, with an ICE hold, deportation proceedings were begun.

It was a double strike: the defendants would serve out a jail or prison term, be released, and then be taken into ICE custody while they went through deportation proceedings. Some prosecutors didn't like the fact that resources were spent on them serving out jail and prison time if they were going to be deported anyway, but she didn't see it that way. They had committed two crimes and deserved two different punishments as far as she was concerned.

She had finished the last of her paperwork, signing probable cause statements in order to get warrants on people who hadn't come to court, when Vince Dale marched into her office. He didn't just walk, he seemed to stomp anywhere he went, as though he had orders from someone and had to carry them out as efficiently as possible.

"Heard Mr. Montgomery didn't show for his prelim," he said, placing his hands on the back of a chair and leaning forward.

"Nope. Brigham genuinely didn't know where he was, either."

"It's a winning situation for us. If he doesn't come back, we basically got a victory without having to put any more resources into it. If he does come back, we can use the fact that he has consciousness of guilt." He grinned. "I wish everybody ran."

"I was looking forward to the trial, honestly."

"Yeah?"

"Yeah. I wanted to watch him while the jury came back with a guilty verdict. See his face."

Vince chuckled. "Wow. Maybe you need to be the one in the boss's chair."

"No, I'm no politician. I just wanna do my job and go home."

He straightened. "Speaking of which, go home. You spend too much time here."

"Don't have to ask me twice."

She logged off her computer and rose. She retrieved her purse and left her office. A few people were randomly milling around, probably trying to show Vince they were the type of attorneys who could stay late. She said goodbye to a couple of them and left the office.

The parking garage was behind the building, and she headed to her car, a black Subaru. As she started the car, talk radio blared through the speakers, and she turned it down before pulling out. As she made her way out of the garage, she saw a red streak on one of the pillars. The streak had been there on her first day, and she remembered thinking to herself that the Salt Lake County DA's office, the most powerful prosecution entity in the state, with the exception of the Attorney General's Office, should at least take enough pride in their parking garage to have it cleaned.

She didn't feel that way anymore. Resources were limited, and budgets seemed to shrink every year rather than expand. Vince was a master at allocating money where it was really needed. Within his first three months in office, he had cut the water coolers, switched everything possible to paperless, switched all the staff to part-time to avoid benefits, and stopped buying snacks for the office. He saved the office nearly $360,000 a year. He used that money to hire two additional prosecutors, and the rest went to resources like in-house investigators and victim advocates.

Cuts continued, and more prosecutors, investigators, and victim advocates were added until all the prosecutors felt they could actually focus on their cases rather than grind away and just try to ease the crushing caseloads. Debra's own caseload had gone from four hundred cases a year to one hundred. She found the deals she was offering to defense attorneys weren't as good because she had no incentive to get rid of cases. She could actually work them as they needed to be worked. And for that reason, she could forgive Vince Dale almost anything else he did. In the end, he cared most about protecting the public.

She took I-15 and got off on 3300 South. The Salt Lake Metro Jail was just up the street, and she parked in the visitor lot. She flashed her district attorney's badge to the clerk.

"Hey, hon," the older woman behind the counter said.

"Everything copasetic, Jaime?"

"Good as can be. He's having dinner right now, but I'll pull him out for you."

"It's past seven. Why's he having dinner now?"

"He was put in ad-seg for a few hours. He got into a fight with another inmate. Over some shaving cream or something like that."

She nodded. "All right, well, I'll talk to him about it."

The doors buzzed, and the heavy metal gate opened. She stepped through and turned right, toward D block. The floors were bare gray cement. Sometimes they hung art from the inmates on the walls, but there was none now. A maintenance crew was working on the track lighting. It seemed out of place to see other people here, talking and laughing as though it were just a normal job at some company.

D block opened, and she stood in the center of a room with six steel doors spread out in front of her. She went to the first door and waited until she heard the click then opened it and stepped inside.

Metal benches sat in front of glass partitions, and she sat down and waited. Most guests weren't allowed phones, wallets, or even coats back here, but she was here so often that they let her slide. It didn't hurt that she worked for the DA's office. She took out her phone and tried to check her email, but there was no reception. Sometimes the signal could get through, and sometimes it couldn't.

A metal door slid open on the other side of the partition, and a guard brought in an older man in an orange jumpsuit. He sat across from her as the guard stepped out and leaned against the railing, looking down on the cells.

"Hey, Pop," she said.

"How are you, darlin'?"

"Not bad. I put more money on your account."

"I know, I saw that. Thanks." He looked down. "Must be so proud of your old man, locked up again."

She shrugged. "Honestly, I never really expected you to get out. You were in and out so much, I thought you'd live here one day."

"Well I'm out in sixty-one days. Just need to figure out where I'm gonna stay."

"You can't stay with me, I'm sorry."

"No, I wasn't implying that—"

"Yes you were."

An image flashed in Debra's mind like a light flicking on and off, but she took in the entire scene: her mother lying on a bedroom floor with a broken nose. She would tell friends and neighbors it happened when she fell somewhere, or that she'd had some surgery. Anything but the truth.

"Well," he said, "maybe I was, a little."

"I'll give you some money to get a motel until you get on your feet. So what's this I hear about you getting into a fight and administrative segregation?"

"It was nothin'. Me and my cellie got into it a little bit. Barely raised our voices."

"Over shaving cream?"

He chuckled. "Ain't nothin' what it seems in here. No, it weren't over shaving cream. That scuffle was a long time comin'."

She nodded. "Do you need anything?"

"No, you've done enough for me." He paused. "I'm sorry your old man's a fuck-up, darlin'. You deserve better."

She exhaled loudly. "Family's family. And you're the only family I got left."

He gave a weak smile and looked away. His eyes glistened as tears began to come and he fought them back.

"I just wanted to check in with you before heading home."

"Do you have to leave now?"

She rose. "Yes. See ya, Pop."

"Take care of yourself, darlin'."

She turned and walked out of the jail without looking back. The sound of the metal doors closing behind her echoed through the halls.

18

The family restaurant served Mexican food and had a waterfall and cliff divers up on a ledge. They dove into the pool while New Age music played.

Timothy led Brigham around the tables and up the stairs to the second floor. Around the corner, at a large circular table, were Ted Montgomery, his three children, and a woman Brigham didn't recognize—Timothy's wife.

"Brigham," Ted said, his face lighting up. "What're you doing here?"

"Can we talk in private?"

"Sure," he said, wiping his lips with a linen napkin. He rose and followed Brigham away from the table to a stone ledge overlooking the pool the divers were splashing into.

"You missed court, Ted."

"I know," he said somberly. "But I had to do a few things."

"It would've taken two hours. You couldn't do them after?"

"These were time-sensitive things. Meetings that I had to attend."

"You can't miss court. I got the judge to hold off on issuing a warrant for twenty-four hours. We've got to appear tomorrow morning and explain to her why you weren't there."

"I know, I put you in an awkward spot. I'm sorry about that. But I'm guessing you've never been facing life in prison. There are things you've got to do to make sure your kids are taken care of."

"If you want to take care of them, show up to court."

He nodded. "I will. I'm sorry." Ted looked back at his kids. "Wanna join us?"

Brigham was starving at this point, but didn't think it appropriate to eat with clients. "No, I better go."

"Nonsense, there's plenty. Come eat."

The food did smell good, and the tight feeling of hunger in his belly made Brigham sit down at the table. He was introduced to Timothy's wife and sat between Ted and Devan.

They were discussing a family they knew back in Oregon. Monica, for the first time since Brigham had met her, was smiling and laughing. The five-year-old, David, seemed to be having a good time as well. Only Devan was staring down at the table with an expressionless face.

"You like the divers?" Brigham said.

He shook his head.

"Why not?"

"I don't know."

Ted had dished out an enchilada and taco and passed it to Brigham, who had to restrain himself to keep from wolfing it down in a few bites. "I always liked running, but not swimming," Brigham said. "I don't think I like being wet."

Devan glanced at him. "I like swimming," he said softly, as if he were revealing too much about himself.

"Yeah? Where do you like to go swimming?"

He folded his arms and kept his eyes on the table. "A pool by our house... my mom used to take me there."

Brigham couldn't speak, and suddenly his appetite wasn't so ravenous. He stared at Devan a few moments, and then put down his fork. Pain sucked at his chest, and he decided he needed to be alone.

"Thanks for the food, Ted," he said.

"What? You barely had two bites."

"That's all I wanted. Nice meeting you folks."

"Okay," Ted said. "Eight thirty tomorrow morning."

"Yes. Don't be late."

Brigham walked off and glanced over his shoulder at the table. Ted was laughing, his arm around Devan. He seemed calm for a man who was facing life in prison. But Brigham had seen all sorts of reactions to the prospect of lengthy incarcerations. One of his clients had overdosed on drugs, another had committed suicide, one had locked herself in her house and knit sweater after sweater until the house was cluttered with them. Maybe relaxing with his family was how Ted dealt with it. At least he'd had the foresight to have some relatives stay with his kids. That would probably be enough to stave off DCFS for a while.

The sky was an off shade of pink as dusk fell. Timothy had given Brigham a ride to the restaurant, with Brigham's bike in the trunk. He had taken it out and locked it to a bike rack. As he got on, he glanced up at the moon, which he could just make out. Checking his cell phone, he saw several text messages and a voicemail. Apparently he hadn't felt them in his pocket.

One was from Molly: *Call me please.*

She answered on the first ring. "Hey," she said.

"Hey."

"I need to see you. You still want dinner?"

"Yup, starving. I'm in Draper, though. Can you meet me at the India House?"

"Be there in ten."

Brigham rode down to the restaurant, a brown building with a pawnshop across the parking lot. The pawnshop had half a car sticking out of the brick wall outside, and he touched it as he passed. The car was real, not a plastic model.

He waited outside until he saw Molly park. He gave her a kiss on the cheek, and they went inside.

"What's so urgent?" he said.

"Let's sit down first."

They were seated by a window. Brigham ordered an appetizer, his stomach growling, and leaned back in the seat as he loosened his tie. "I found Ted. He was—"

"Brigham, I have to tell you something. And you're not going to like it."

"That's a weird way to start a conversation."

"I'm serious. This… is serious."

"Okay, what's going on?"

She swallowed. "Vince Dale has been offering me positions at the DA's office all year. And I've turned him down. About a month ago, he offered again. I didn't turn him down. I accepted two days ago."

Brigham was quiet for a time long enough to be awkward. "You're quitting?"

She nodded. "I'm sorry. I just feel it's the right move."

"Wait a second. You're quitting your own firm… to work for Vince Dale?"

"You say that with such hatred. I don't think he's what you think he is."

"Are you fucking kidding me? He's everything that's vile and soulless in our profession."

"Keep your voice down." She glanced around to see if anyone was watching. "I've known him a lot longer than you. He does what he thinks is right, and sometimes that rubs people the wrong way."

He shook his head. "I don't believe it. We've just become successful, and you're gonna bail on us? You helped build this firm into what it is. How can you leave it to be some government stooge?"

"I won't be a stooge," she said, irritated. "He's putting me in Special Prosecutions. The high-profile division. I'll have autonomy."

"No, you won't. You don't understand men like Vince Dale. I know them, I know them really well. My father was one of them. You can never have autonomy with a guy like him. It will always be about the power he has over you. Nothing else will matter to him."

"I think you're wrong."

He stared out the windows at the passing traffic. "What is this about? Really? Don't lie, either, I don't deserve that."

"I wasn't going to lie. I just don't think defense is a good fit for me."

"What're you talking about? You're great at it."

"Being good at something doesn't mean it's a good fit for you."

Brigham gazed at her, his eyes catching hers and not letting them go. He had so much anger that he didn't know how to express it without ruining their relationship forever. But the anger was only the surface. Something much deeper hurt, and he couldn't put his finger on what it was. Betrayal maybe, though he didn't know what exactly she was betraying. "It's about that chi mo, isn't it? Because his victim killed himself? You had nothing to do with that. You had no control over it happening in the first place—the acquittal, or the suicide. That had nothing to do with you. Your job is to defend the Constitution. That's what we're fighting for, not individual clients."

"I know… but I'm not sure I believe that anymore. I helped him. And I know that another lawyer might've done the exact same thing and everything would've ended up the exact same way, but it wasn't another lawyer. It was me. *I* got him off. And that kid preferred dying over living with the prospect of that monster walking around free."

"That's what we do, Molly," he said quietly. "You need both sides fighting hard, and somehow you get a close approximation of the truth sometimes. Sometimes monsters go free, and sometimes innocent people go to prison. That's the system. But giving yourself over to someone like Vince Dale is not the answer."

She chuckled. "You make him sound like the devil."

"Do you have any proof he's not?"

"Brigham—"

"I'm sure he's fine to work for. A lot of my buddies at the DA's office say he has their backs and gets them whatever resources they need. I'm talking about something deeper. His operational philosophy, I guess. His view of people. It's not your view of people, and I'm scared of him infecting you with that nihilism."

She reached out and gently placed her hand over his. "I've known Vince almost a decade, and if anything, I influence him. Not the other way around."

He sighed. "I hope you're right. But I'm not sure you are."

He took her hand in his. All the anger, the betrayal, and the pain faded with a simple touch. Some women had that power over men, or at least over him. When his mother would do something he didn't like and he was in a rage as a teenager, she would simply put her arms around him and kiss his forehead and everything dark would flow out of him. Molly had that same effect.

"I..." she said.

"I know. Me, too."

19

Brigham was at the Matheson Courthouse at eight in the morning. He paced around the lobby, looking up at the statue of a man holding a briefcase, the Matheson paterfamilias. He stared at the building's decorated dome for a while then chatted with an attorney he'd met a few months back. Mostly, he worried that Ted wasn't going to show up again today. The judge would issue an arrest warrant, and there was no way anyone would be able to get him out again until the case was over.

Ted arrived at 8:27 a.m. and hurried over to Brigham. "Sorry."

"Let's go," Brigham said, rushing him to the metal detectors. Brigham had set the appointment yesterday, and the judge had no other cases this morning. If he wasn't there when she took the bench, she might leave.

He was pulled to the side and wanded, asked to take off his shoes, and wanded again. Ted was allowed right through.

They walked in just as the judge was taking the bench. Brigham hurried to the lectern and didn't say anything, hoping the judge wouldn't either. She just smiled, a smile that told him he had cut it too close, and then said, "Let's call the matter of

Ted Montgomery. Mr. Montgomery is represented by Mr. Brigham Theodore and Ms. Debra Flynn is here for the State."

Ted stood next to Brigham as the judge flipped through her file. He whispered, "I want the quickest trial date possible."

"We have to have a preliminary hearing," Brigham whispered back, moving the microphone away from them. "Then I'm going to file motions challenging a few things. After all that, we'll have motions in limine and then set a jury trial."

He shook his head. "No, I want a trial. I don't need all that stuff."

Brigham was silent a moment. "What're you talking about, Ted? All that *stuff* is what the law is about. After five or six motions and rulings on the evidence, this case could look very different."

"I get that, but we're not gonna win on that stuff, are we? You know it, and I know it. This is about the jury and their emotions. For that, we need a trial. And I don't want to be in limbo the next two years. I want the first date the judge has."

"Your Honor," Brigham said, "I'm sorry, could I just have a second with my client?"

"Certainly."

Brigham took his arm and led him out past the double doors. "You can't be serious."

"I've thought about this a lot. Since before I came to see you. I don't want to play around. I don't have the stomach for it." He looked through the windows into the courtroom. "I've been through about as much pain as a husband can go through. I just don't have it in me, Brigham. I want this decided one way or the other as quickly as possible. And if the cards go against me, I know my kids will have their auntie and uncle at least. Please, do this for me."

Brigham shook his head. "The soonest we could get in is two weeks from now."

"That's what I want."

"Ted, it takes me longer than that to prepare for a DUI trial. There are months of investigation we need done and then months more of motions and hearings. We can't rush this. It'll get screwed up."

"I know the risks. And I know you're good at your job, and you will do the best you can with what you have. But this is eating away at me, at all of us. I need it over with. Please."

Brigham looked at the judge, who appeared to be surfing the Internet. Debra was tapping her pen against a yellow legal pad and staring off into space. The sole bailiff in the room was playing on his phone, and the judge's clerk was eating something out of a plastic bowl. It was so casual for them, just another day at the office. But he was the one who had Ted's life in his hands. If he did this wrong, Ted would die in prison, and his kids would grow up without either parent. The four people in the courtroom didn't have that pressure.

"Okay," he said softly. "I'll do what you're asking me. But it's a mistake."

"Thank you."

They reentered the courtroom and this time walked calmly to the lectern. Brigham stood for a moment without speaking while Judge Lawrence finished what she was doing online and turned to him.

"Your Honor, Mr. Montgomery was unaware of the serious nature of missing a court date yesterday. He is here now and ready to move forward. We would ask the Court not to take him into custody, simply to admonish him."

Debra rose to her feet. "Your Honor, this is a murder case. He's clearly not taking this seriously. I would ask that he be taken into custody without bail until the resolution of this case."

"His wife of nineteen years begged for him to end her pain. Believe me, Your Honor, he takes it seriously."

The judge nodded and took a few breaths before speaking. "Mr. Montgomery, someone was generous enough to pay fifty thousand dollars to secure your release—money that could've been forfeited yesterday for nothing. Please show up to court on time when you're scheduled. I don't want to hold you in jail if I don't have to, and I'm sure the family member who put that money up doesn't want to have it mean nothing."

"Won't happen again, Your Honor," Ted said.

"Okay, well, see that it doesn't." She turned to her computer. "And the next available date for preliminary hearing is—"

"Your Honor," Brigham interrupted, "we would actually ask that this… that this be set directly for jury trial."

The judge's brow furrowed. "You want to go from initial appearance to jury trial?"

"Yes. Mr. Montgomery will be waiving his preliminary hearing rights."

The judge looked to Ted. "Mr. Montgomery, is this what you want?"

"Yes."

"And what has your counsel advised you about the decision?"

"He told me not to do it."

The judge shook her head. "I would tend to agree with him. You need to give him time to do his job."

"My attorney is excellent, Your Honor. But this is my decision. I want to waive my preliminary hearing rights and just have a jury trial. Please."

The judge shrugged. "Ms. Flynn, when could you be ready?"

"I need to subpoena my witnesses, so at least two weeks."

The judge looked at Brigham and, reluctantly, he nodded.

"Two weeks it is, the twenty-first then. Eight sharp, Mr.

Montgomery. Please fill out the waiver the bailiff has for you."

The form was brought over, and Ted filled it out and handed it back. The judge looked at both attorneys and said, "Anything else?"

"No, Your Honor."

"Nothing Your Honor."

"Okay, court is adjourned."

As they walked out of the courtroom, Brigham turned to his client and said, "You sure about this?"

"Yes. Thank you for respecting my wishes."

He nodded. "I just hope your wishes don't land you in prison for the rest of your life."

20

The first thing Brigham did when he got back was to go to Molly's office. It was empty except for the desk, chair, and computer. She'd already left. He hadn't expected it so fast. He'd spent the night with her last night, and they hadn't talked about exactly when it would be happening. She had her clients, too, but the paralegals were notifying them that either Scotty or Rebecca was taking over for her.

"Hey," Rebecca said, walking by in the hall.

"Hey."

"So that's crazy, huh?"

"It is."

Rebecca adjusted her glasses. "Not everyone can do everything. You have to go with what you like."

He nodded. "Yeah. You missed Ted's hearing this morning."

"Oh, sorry. I inherited like thirty cases from Molly."

"I understand. But I need your help now. The trial's in two weeks."

"That seems fast."

"It is fast, the fastest I've ever had to prepare for any trial. The first thing we need to do is get our investigator to dig up as much as she can about the witnesses and then interview them. I've interviewed a lot of them, but we need a third party to do it. When we have her reports, we can follow up with any questions we have for the witnesses. Then we have to prep Ted for his testimony. I also want his daughter to testify. We'll have to touch base with her. But the biggest question right now is where he got the morphine to do it. He won't tell me."

"Why not?"

"I don't know. Sometimes clients are scared that their own lawyer can turn them or their accomplices in. Schedule a time for him to come in and prep with me, and I'll explain attorney–client privilege more clearly. For now, call Jen, our investigator, and get her going on everything else. Tell her I really, really need to know how he got the morphine. Also make sure there wasn't some large life insurance policy taken out before Ruby's death or anything. That's the last thing we need the prosecutor to put into the jurors' minds."

"I'm on it," she said, heading off.

Brigham glanced into Molly's office one more time before going to his own. He sat in his chair and opened his calendar. He had a couple of client meetings that day, one court appearance in a small court in a city named Bountiful, and then nothing the rest of the afternoon. He leaned his head back on the chair and decided he'd stare at the ceiling until his first client consult came in.

137

Normally, when he had a few minutes, he would go to Molly's office.

He sighed and put his feet up on the desk.

21

The parking garage was half full as Molly parked. Her stomach was a bundle of nervous energy, and she hoped that would fade as the day wore on. She wasn't used to being nervous.

As she walked through the garage to get to the walkway that would take her into the main building, she noticed a red streak across one of the support pillars. It looked like spray paint or possibly house paint, and she wondered why no one had removed it.

The walkway overlooked the busy street below, and she had to stop a moment and stare down at the morning crowds rushing into the office buildings. Granted, she had lived in San Francisco and Los Angeles, and by comparison, Salt Lake City was barely populated. But there were still enough people that, stepping back, the number of people crammed into a single city overwhelmed her.

She entered the building and stopped. This was it, she thought. No going back now.

Her office was past the metal detectors. She hadn't been given an ID or badge yet and had to present her driver's license to the receptionist who buzzed her in. A slim woman with too much makeup came over to her and removed her eyeglasses.

"You're Molly Becker?"

"Yes."

"I'm Helen. I'll be showing you around. Follow me."

Molly was taken on a tour of the DA's offices, or at least her floor. They stopped at each office, and Helen introduced her. The person inside, usually sitting at a desk, would have to stop what they were doing and say hello. It felt awkward and forced, like having to introduce herself to the class on the first day of school. She wished she could just meet everyone, some of whom she already knew, on her own time.

"This is your office," Helen finally said after they'd done the rounds for twenty minutes. "Don't know what Vince has for you, but we need these probable-cause statements written."

Sitting on the desk were stacks of files, each of them blue with a tag on the front that read: Homeless.

"Are these all homeless people?" Molly asked.

"Yup. They pee on the train or the bus, stuff like that. You gotta write a probable-cause statement to issue a warrant for 'em, 'cause they never come to court. Lemme know when you're done with that, and then I'll have some other things for you."

Molly sat down at her desk and stared quietly at the stack of files. With a sigh, she turned on the computer and opened the first file.

Three hours ground away as slowly as she could've imagined. Each probable-cause statement was the same, and seemingly for the same crimes. The homeless would either be cited for sleeping in Pioneer Park or cited for riding Trax without a ticket. Occasionally there was a clearly mentally ill defendant who urinated on Trax or defecated in front of a fast-food restaurant, but for the most part, Molly got the sense that the police were trying to harass the homeless enough to get them to go elsewhere.

She finished the statements but didn't tell anyone. She wanted a moment to herself, mostly to contemplate whether she'd made the worst mistake of her life in coming here. It had been a gut reaction to something emotional. Had she really reasoned this out? Was she going to retire at the DA's office? Writing PC statements to have schizophrenic homeless people arrested for riding on a public train without a ticket? She shuddered and wondered if Brigham would respect her less if she came back.

Deciding she needed a break, she wandered out into the hall. Just to get familiar with the place, she re-walked the route Helen had taken her on and then rode the elevator to another floor. The DA's office put different divisions on different floors, and she stepped off onto the floor for the civil division:

the section that dealt with anything other than criminal matters.

There weren't as many attorneys in the civil division as in the criminal one, and as opposed to the criminal division, music was blaring in almost everyone's office. She figured it was because Vince and the other chief prosecutors probably never came down to the civil division.

Satisfied that there was less here than on her floor, Molly got back onto the elevator and went to a different floor. This one was more elegantly decorated, with lots of glass and nice paintings on the walls. She realized when she saw a receptionist that she wasn't on a DA floor any longer but a law firm's. She smiled at the secretary and was about to head back to the elevator when she heard a male voice say, "Molly?"

She turned to see a man in a black suit with a pink tie. His hair was combed to the side, and a gold pin held his tie in place.

"Jack?" she said, walking over to him.

"Hey, how are you?" he said, placing an arm over her shoulders.

She hugged him back. "Good. I haven't seen you since the graduation party."

"I know. I mean, I see your Facebook posts and stuff, but we've never hung out. We definitely have to."

"Well, I'm closer now, so anytime you want to."

"Where you at?"

"The DA's office."

"Really? Wow, that's gotta be interesting. Those guys are always rushing everywhere."

"So far I've had about a hundred homeless people arrested. Not exactly glamorous. But look at you, at the big white-shoe law firm."

He grinned bashfully. "I'm one of the partners now. Well, we call them shareholders for liability reasons, but it's the same thing."

"That's great. Good for you."

"Yeah… hey, what're you doing for lunch?"

"Nothing."

"There's this awesome Chinese place just down the street. You in?"

She shrugged. "I don't really have anything else going on. Why not?"

22

Brigham sat across from Rebecca at their conference room table, both of them poring over documents on Lexis, the legal research program. They were reading case law in Utah and the surrounding area for a case similar to Ted's. Brigham needed to know what had been tried before and, particularly, what had worked and what hadn't.

As his old boss Tommy had told him, the jury may want to acquit, but if they didn't get a reason, they wouldn't do it. They had to have something they could tell their spouses when they got home, and not that they'd just let a potential murderer go free. The reason had to be enough to convince the spouse that their significant other had acted properly. And that's all Brigham wanted: a decent reason to let Ted Montgomery go.

He wasn't that great at legal research. That and legal writing had bored him to tears and had been his worst subjects. He had always preferred arguing something in front of someone, whether that someone was a judge or a jury. He felt he was best when he was on his feet and caught off guard.

He was glad Rebecca was there. She was, in many ways, his legal opposite. Not bad at speaking, but far superior to him at research and writing.

"I think I found something," she said.

"What?"

"*State of Utah v. Logom.* It's a Supreme Court case from 1958."

Brigham leaned back in his chair, happy to push the laptop away from him. "Yikes. What's it say?"

She scanned the case. "Logom suffocated his wife with a pillow. It came out at trial that she was suffering from tuberculosis, and the doctors had said she was a hopeless case. They said she'd feel immense pain before death, and there was nothing they could do. He took the stand and testified that she was in constant pain and begging him to end her life. His wife specifically asked him to suffocate her with the pillow, because she'd go quickly. The trial court didn't let the defense present testimony that his wife had said that, saying it was unreliable hearsay because the party who said it wasn't available to testify, and the defense appealed. The Court of Appeals affirmed, but when it got to the Supreme Court, they overturned and said that it was relevant to his defense of temporary insanity and indicated the reliability of the hearsay based on the totality of the circumstances. They remanded for a new trial, and Logom was acquitted by a jury."

"Temporary insanity, huh? Does that ever work?"

She shrugged. "I've seen it work on *Law & Order.*"

Brigham chuckled. "We're a shoo-in, then." He put his feet up on the table and stared at the ceiling. "Temporary insanity doesn't mean a person's insane, it means they were insane for that particular circumstance and it was caused by external factors. I think the better route is diminished capacity. We have to show that he was incapable of forming the intent to commit murder, and so he only caused the death recklessly. It would reduce it to manslaughter or maybe even negligent homicide if we can get the jury to buy it."

"That doesn't really get him off, though."

"Criminal law is just damage control. You're trying to pick the least-worst option. I've never even heard of temporary insanity working with a Utah jury. Diminished capacity works some of the time, I think because the defendant isn't acquitted. The jury feels like they reached a good compromise."

She rested her jaw on her hand and stared absently at the laptop screen before she nodded and said, "I think you're right."

"Diminished capacity it is, then. Let's get all the homicide cases that have used it in the past few years. We need transcripts if any of them have gone to trial."

"In two weeks? Can we get them that fast?"

"Not really. But maybe we can pay a little more and they'll do a rush order for us."

"I'm on it," she said, rising and heading out of the room.

"And Rebecca?"

"Yeah?" she said, turning around.

"Thanks for your help. It's kind of a weird time here right now."

She hesitated. "She's crazy to leave. It's awesome here."

He grinned. "Thanks."

The bulk of the day was spent going to court on cases and doing interviews. Brigham interviewed ten attorneys to fill Molly's spot. The only one he liked was a former bodybuilder who specialized in motions and legal writing. He seemed shy for a bodybuilder and had a tough time looking Brigham in the eye. His name was Gerald Trudaux, and he spoke with a heavy accent. Brigham asked him how many languages he spoke.

"Seven," he said.

"You're French, aren't you?"

"Yes. But my heart is American. I love war and pornography."

Brigham laughed. "We have a few other things in our culture, I think."

"I know," he said with a smile. "Your Constitution is the greatest monument to man's mind in history. It's a shame no one understands it. It will soon not hold strength in the culture and be done away with."

"Why do you say that?"

"When a thing is taken for granted, people believe they can abolish it without consequence. That's what happened in my country during the Revolution."

Instantly, Brigham liked him. For the second time, he hired someone on the spot.

The firm had enough attorneys now that he could hand the minor cases off to Rebecca and Gerald and focus on Ted's trial. Brigham didn't mind doing things on the fly. In fact he preferred it. But two weeks to prepare for a murder trial was unheard of. And if Ted was convicted and regretted his decision, then the typical grounds for appeal—ineffective assistance of counsel—might not be available because he was the one who chose to go quickly against his counsel's advice.

Brigham explored the case law Rebecca had provided. No trials similar had been held in Utah. He found that hard to believe, so he did his own search and she was correct. A trial like this had no precedent in this state.

Diminished capacity wasn't a defense he had used before, so he read everything he could find that discussed it. The theory was simple: due to a mental disorder or other affliction, the defendant was unable to fully appreciate the nature of his actions and form the requisite intent to commit the crime alleged. Then you presented the jury with a lesser-included offense and asked them to convict. It was similar to what

Brigham had done in the Amanda Pierce trial, except that Brigham didn't present the jury with several alternatives and the jury didn't need to find Ted insane; only that, at the time, he didn't have his full mental faculties.

The theory was simple enough, but proving it seemed impossible. He would have to have a psychiatrist do an evaluation of Ted in the next week to determine what his state of mind was at the time of the offense. It was like trying to determine what the weather had been like last month based on what it was that day. But with the hourly rate he would be paying, he was certain he could find somebody to do it. And that's all he needed: someone with the right credentials to get up there and say Ted hadn't committed murder because his mental state was such that he didn't know what he was doing. Since experts couldn't make ultimate judgements in front of the jury, they would have to be skilled enough to convey that sentiment without actually saying it.

His phone rang and it was Jen, his private investigator. "Give me something good, Jen."

"Well, first, I'm sorry to hear about Molly. I really liked her."

"She's not dead. She's just working somewhere else."

"I know. And actually prosecutors and defense attorneys make perfect couples. The jobs are similar enough to talk about over dinner but dissimilar enough that it's interesting for the other person."

"Yeah. It was just sort of out of the blue, though. I wish she would've talked to me about it first. But she's independent that way. It wouldn't have mattered what I had to say."

"That's what makes her who she is."

He exhaled and leaned back in his chair, glancing out into the hallway as one of the paralegals passed by on her cell phone. "What about Ted?"

"Well, there is a life insurance policy, three million, but it was taken out seven years ago, six years before she got the cancer, and it was taken out on both of them. It was a renewal from a policy they already had, so, I doubt the prosecutor will even bring it up."

"No, he didn't do this for money. I almost wish he had. That I could understand. I don't understand killing your wife because of a disease."

"Really? You don't understand it?"

Brigham hesitated. "She might've lived."

"Maybe. Don't judge a person until you walk in their shoes."

A pang of guilt climbed down his gut as if he'd swallowed ice. "What else?"

"He's well respected at his work as a mechanical engineer. He works in something called structured systems. Not sure what that is. But apparently you have to be really smart to do it."

"Really? I didn't get a brainiac vibe from him."

"Super-smart people don't show off that they're smart, I think. He's got his PhD in engineering, and he was a professor at the University of Oregon before taking a position at this robotics company out here. He's been married once before. I couldn't get ahold of his ex, and she didn't return any of my calls. I looked up the divorce petition and it just said irreconcilable differences."

"Huh. Standard stuff. Anything good for us?"

"No criminal history whatsoever. I mean, nothing. Not even a speeding ticket. The guy's as clean as they come."

Brigham stretched his neck to the side. He'd found that the more he sat, the more aches and pains would manifest throughout his body. He wondered if he was just getting older, or if these were the consequences of a more sedentary life. "What about the morphine?"

"I interviewed the doctor and a few nurses. I know you talked to a couple, but I got some good stuff from some of the others. I'm gonna shoot those summaries over to you now. The main nurse, the one the State is calling, is pretty damaging. Ted and his kids were there and she was alive, the nurse came back later and the wife was dead. The wife had a morphine drip the nurse hadn't set up, and the bag wasn't from the hospital. He didn't get it there, so they think he must've brought it with him."

"Where would a guy like Ted, with no criminal connections, get a bag of morphine?"

"Who knows?"

"I'm trying to argue diminished capacity—that he did this recklessly because he was so distraught. If he went out and bought morphine weeks before and then brought it to the hospital, that's gonna be a deal breaker for the jury."

"Sorry to be the bearer of bad news. Maybe if you get him to flip on the dealer, the DA would give you a better deal."

"No, the prosecutor's really adamant about this one."

"Who is it?"

"Debra Flynn."

"Oh."

"What?" he said, opening his email to see how many he had to read after this conversation.

"I've seen her in trial. She's good. Totally thorough. She had this great piece of evidence she had given to the defense attorney in a stack of other evidence and knew he hadn't looked at it. So she didn't mention it the entire trial. Then she waited for closing. During rebuttal, she brought it up. It was brilliant."

Rebuttal closing. Brigham had cringed when he had first learned that the prosecutor got to give two closing arguments. The prosecution spoke first, then the defense gave their closing, and then the prosecution got to speak again. To withhold mentioning damaging evidence until rebuttal meant the defense could not respond to it. It was a brilliant strategy.

"Wow. I wouldn't even think to do that."

"That's what I'm saying," she said. "Be careful with her."

"I will."

"I'll shoot over the reports. There's some more in there, but that was the most important stuff."

"Thanks, Jen. Call me if you find anything else."

Brigham hung up and checked the clock on his phone. He wondered if he could catch Ted now and maybe get him off guard so he wouldn't be prepared for Brigham's questions. Ted was probably at home at this hour, but Brigham had no idea.

He rose and headed out of the office to find his client.

23

No one answered at Ted's home, at first. Brigham was about to give up and leave when Monica opened the door. She seemed different now, more cheery. She'd been pale and melancholy, and that had lifted.

"Hi, Monica."

"Hi."

"Your dad home?"

"No."

"Any idea where I can find him?"

"Um, no."

"Your uncle home?"

She glanced away, sheepishly looking down at her feet. "No."

Brigham noticed something. The mention of her uncle made her uncomfortable. "I really need to speak to your dad. Do you have any idea where he could've gone?"

"He sometimes goes to the coffee shop and plays chess with people."

"Up on Fremont? The Coffee Chalk, I think, right?"

"Yeah."

"Okay, well, I'll try up there. Thanks."

Monica was hiding something. It had to do with her uncle, and it was something she clearly didn't want him to know. Then again, since when were teenagers predictable? Her mother had just died and her father was facing life in prison for killing her. Brigham decided he shouldn't be so quick to judge.

Coffee Chalk was only a few blocks away, and Brigham secured his bike and went inside. The smell of baking pastries and brewing coffee always comforted him. In law school, he never went to bars or restaurants; he was always at coffee shops studying or commiserating with other law students.

He scanned the first floor and didn't see Ted. He took the stairs up and searched there. At a table by the window, Ted was sitting by himself sipping a frothy drink. He had a Mac open but was staring out the window.

"Good coffee?" Brigham said.

Ted showed a trace of surprise, but it lasted only a moment and then faded away. "Not really. But the lattes are good. You want one?"

Brigham sat down across from him. "No. I came to speak to you about something."

"Must be important if you tracked me down at a coffee shop."

He leaned forward, ensuring that no one at any of the nearby tables could hear. "I need to know where the morphine came from."

"I told you, I can't tell you."

"Why?"

"It's just something I can't share. I'm sorry."

"Even though I can't tell anyone else, and if I do, it can't be used against you?"

"Yes. I just can't risk it."

"Can you risk life in prison?"

He sipped his drink and replaced the cup on the table. Outside, a Trax train sped by the empty stop. "I can't. I'm sorry. Look, I know I've made your job exponentially more difficult, but this is the way I want this handled. It *has* to be handled this way."

"It's clear you're protecting someone, and I get that. They probably did you a favor getting you that morphine. But just tell me. I need to know. That's all. I just want to *know*. I won't act on it if you don't want me to. But I can't be surprised in the courtroom and find out who it was in the middle of your trial when the prosecutor brings it out."

Ted nodded. "Do you have any kids?"

Brigham paused. He wasn't getting through. He leaned back in his seat. "No, I don't."

"They're the best part of life. It's our way of being immortal. I mean, if you don't believe in God. I'm not religious, myself. Are you?"

"Religious, no. But I believe in God."

"Ruby was religious. We would have heated debates about it because she wanted the kids to go to church, and I thought it was a waste of time. She'd try and slip spirituality into my life. I'd open my car door and a Bible or a copy of the teachings of Buddha would be on my seat. Sometimes for our movie night she'd sneak in a movie she knew was about people finding God and peace. I hated those movies. But I'd watch them because I knew she thought she was being clever." He looked out the windows again. "I miss her. I miss her so much that sometimes it feels like a part of me is gone. Like I've had a limb amputated or something, and I can still feel it. Then when I look for it, it's like I feel that pain all over again." He looked Brigham in the eyes. "If there was any way I could've saved her, I would've done it. Even if it would've cost me my life, my work, everything. I would've done it to save her."

Brigham nodded. "I get that feeling from you."

"So you have to believe me when I say I can't tell you who got me that morphine. It just… I can't do it. Not to them."

"Okay," he said with a sigh. "Okay. Well, we'll do it with a lot of unknowns then. But you have to realize, if the prosecutor has more information than I do, she will use it, and we'll be caught with our pants down. I can only defend what I know about."

"I know. And I'm sorry to put you in this situation."

Brigham scanned the coffee shop. He saw groups of college students studying and a few older men playing chess. One pair looked like they were on a date. The demographic hadn't changed at all.

"Why did you choose me for this case, Ted?" Brigham asked.

"Someone at work dropped your name, but I also read about that murder case you defended last year. I remembered it in the news. I was really impressed."

"You shouldn't be. I have no idea how we got that verdict."

"You got that verdict because you understand people. I knew you'd understand me."

Brigham rose. "We're going to have you come into the office so I can prepare your testimony. Let's do that in the next few days."

He nodded. "Thanks, Brigham. For understanding."

"Don't forget that gratitude if we lose."

24

Brigham was surprised how little he actually had to do once someone like Rebecca was in the office. She was a whirlwind of efficiency. She organized the cases they had by court and then called each individual prosecutor and court and rescheduled the hearings so they could stack four or five cases at once. She worked out deals with the prosecutors over the phone ahead of time. Brigham's calendar was so clear that he could spend his time on Ted's case without missing anything else.

For several days, he and Rebecca read any case they could find on diminished capacity, which wasn't much. They even called an attorney Brigham had befriended and asked his advice, going through a few scenarios with him. But it turned out he was just as clueless as they were. "In twenty-five years of practice," he said, "I've never had to use that defense in a murder case."

Brigham read the reports submitted by his private investigator, and they were pretty much what he expected. The doctor was called in afterward and confirmed the death after attempting to revive Ruby.

The nurse would be first to testify, then the doctor, then

the detective, and finally the medical examiner. The State also notified him that half a dozen other hospital staff could be called.

On his end, he had Monica and Ted. The private investigator hadn't found anybody else that had relevant information. Monica and Ted were the only two people who had ever heard Ruby ask for someone to kill her.

Preparing Ted had been easy. Brigham didn't want to go through too many questions, or even the actual ones he would be asking. The jury, he felt, could see through too much preparation. He wanted Ted's responses authentic.

Monica, on the other hand, had trouble getting two words out. She would only say "yes" or "no" wherever possible, and Brigham had to drag her testimony out of her, sentence by sentence. It was understandable, considering everything she'd been through. He wouldn't want to relive it all in front of strangers, either.

The day was exhausting, though in reality he'd done nothing more than sit at his desk and read cases and talk with people. He had begun preparing his opening when he remembered that his IT guy had downloaded all the videos Monica had taken. He closed his legal research portal and opened the first file.

The first video must've been taken early in the progression of Ruby Montgomery's disease. She was smiling and playing with her children, wearing jeans and a blouse, still an outpatient. Ted wasn't there.

He flipped to the next video. In this one, she was still at home, but something was different. She appeared pale and listless. He watched the video for a while. David attempted to play with her, but she brushed him away. There were several videos like that. And then he got to the first one of her hospitalized.

Monica, holding her cell phone with the camera on, walked into her mother's hospital room. Ruby was staring out the window. She had lost weight and seemed to have aged a decade, though it'd probably been only months. Turning her head slowly, she took in her children and smiled a weak smile. The children swarmed around her, not realizing their mother was too frail to respond. Ted was there in this one, and he sat across from her, working on his phone while the children played. He and his wife didn't speak five words to each other.

Brigham pictured long nights talking about her death. Talking and talking and talking, until there was nothing left to say. Each accepted the hand fate had dealt them and had emotionally shut down.

Several of the videos were good examples to show to the jury, and Brigham attached them to emails and sent them to one of the paralegals, asking her to burn two discs and send one to the prosecutor. He then closed the media player and rose. The key video that he would attempt to play for the jury several times would be the video Monica had shown him. The one of Ruby asking Ted to end her life. It was painful to watch, but he'd have to play it as much as he could so the jury understood what choice Ted had had in front of him.

His eyes hurt, and a headache had started at the front of his skull and was working its way back.

He decided to call it a day and headed out. Scotty was flirting with one of their secretaries up front and followed him out to the elevators.

"You okay?" he said.

"Fine, why?" Brigham asked.

"Because you look tired."

"I am tired."

"And you look like someone killed your pet turtle since Molly left."

He shook his head. "It was so fast. She dumped us like she didn't even know us. She told me about it after she accepted the position."

"Have you seen her since then?"

"No. I've been letting her calls go to voicemail."

"You can't do that."

The elevator dinged and opened. Brigham rolled his bike on and pushed the button for the bottom floor. "Why not?"

"Because we're each fighting our own battles and need

help sometimes. Even her."

The doors shut, and Brigham was left staring at his reflection in the polished steel. The elevators stopped on one other floor and a couple got on. They were groping each other and laughing, sharing kisses and then glancing back to him to see if he was watching. He kept his eyes on the numbers above the door.

When they got off the elevator, he waited until they had left the building and then stood in the lobby for a minute. He rolled his bike over to the wall and leaned it there as he took a seat. The entrance was mostly glass, and he could see the bank across the street and the enormous amount of traffic between the buildings on Main Street.

Finally, after about ten minutes, he sighed, rose, and headed out the entrance.

25

Jennifer Vest sat in her office until the sun had set and night overtook the city. She had stripped off her jacket and sat in a sleeveless shirt, exposing the tattoos that ran from her shoulder to her wrist on her right arm. She had begun the collection while growing up in the barrio in East Los Angeles. A tattoo shop near where she'd lived hadn't asked for identification, and she and her friends had started getting tattoos there at thirteen.

Back then, she was Jennifer Alvarez. At thirteen, she had an impending sense of her own doom: she would never leave the barrio alive.

Being in a gang wasn't optional. She could either be part of a gang or their victim. She saw too many girls beat up or worse every day because they didn't join. Sometimes they got invited to parties and then were drugged by the girls and given to the guys to gang rape. The girls in the gangs thought that hilarious. Jennifer never took part in that, but every moment, she was scheming and plotting some way to get out of the barrio.

Her mother worked in a factory from sunup to sundown, and she had no idea who her father was. Her mother had told her he was an army man she'd met when she was younger. He'd promised her the moon and the stars, but when she got pregnant, he was gone.

At fifteen, Jennifer discovered the beauty of fake IDs. Her friends used them to get into bars, but she had another purpose for them: work. She started at fifteen and saved every penny. By the time she was seventeen, she had enough saved up to get her and her mother out of the barrio and into a decent apartment in Brentwood—away from her so-called friends and the gang.

Technically, she had to be jumped out of a gang or else she wouldn't be considered to have left. When she was considering informing them and asking to be jumped out, they said they had some work for her. A rival gang member was talking shit, they told her, and she needed to get wet. "Getting wet" was what they called killing someone because of the amount of blood that poured out.

Jennifer knew it was time. She packed up and moved her mother in one day and didn't tell anyone—not her school, not her friends, not even other family members.

She earned her GED and decided to join the police force. It was the only option she thought made sense for her. She knew she didn't have the study skills to excel in academia, but she did excel on the force. She was detective in less than four years and in Robbery-Homicide in another two.

The hours were what forced her out. When she was on

call, there were times she would work thirty or forty hours straight, sleep a few hours, and then get called out on another case. For someone who wanted a husband and children, it wasn't a lifestyle she could maintain.

When she met her husband and he convinced her they should move to Utah, the final pieces were in place and, for the first time in her life, she knew she'd truly pulled herself out of the barrio.

Her cell phone buzzed on her desk, and she noticed for the first time that it was past eight. She answered.

"Ramon," she said, "little early for you to be awake. Parties don't start until ten."

"Shit, I been up since morning. Running game on these bitches."

She grinned. "What'd you need?"

"Word was you needed some dirt on that fuckin' pig. Sean."

"Detective Henry Sean?"

"Yeah."

"What about him?"

"I got some dirt, chiquita."

"What kinda dirt?"

He chuckled. "The kind you wanna buy. Come down and see the homies."

"Don't waste my time, Ramon."

"I ain't."

"All right. See ya in a few."

Her car, a black Cadillac CTS, was parked out in front of her building. She'd founded Investigations International with her husband, himself an ex-FBI agent in the terrorism task force. The company had grown when they branched out into bodyguards and began offering security details to celebrities during the Sundance Film Festival. As their reputation grew, they were hired full time for actors and actresses, musicians, and even a few politicians overseas. The building, once rented, was now hers as well.

She didn't have to do this part of it. If she wanted to, she could sit in her office and be an administrator. There was no need for her to do any investigation, and in fact, she'd cut back to no more than a handful of cases a year. But whenever Brigham called, she answered. She wasn't exactly sure what he struck her as, but it was something she didn't see in a lot of other clients. He was kind, cared in a way about everyone, and she enjoyed being around that. He didn't seem to judge people for what they did, knowing that in similar circumstances, anyone might do the same thing. She loved that about him.

Ramon lived in West Valley, about twenty minutes from her office. He was one of her many contacts. When she needed information about cops, she didn't go to the cops. She knew they protected their own as much as they could. She went to the street. The true gangsters kept tabs on the cops in their territories. Ramon knew every detective in the Narcs unit by first name and had at least seen every other detective in Robbery-Homicide, Vice, and Special Victims. They were enemies, and Ramon didn't like to fight his enemies blind.

She stopped in front of the house and looked in. Several rough-looking Hispanic men were sitting on the porch drinking, thumping bass coming from inside the house. Jen walked up the steps and through them as though they weren't there, showing no fear. They made a few disgusting comments, but she wasn't worried. They knew what Ramon would do if they touched her.

Inside, people were lying around on the couches, watching television and smoking joints. She crossed the living room and saw Ramon at a table in the kitchen with two other men, playing cards.

"What's up, chiquita?"

"Let's talk."

Ramon tossed his cards on the table and rose. He walked out the back door, and she followed him. Outside was a large, unkempt yard strewn with all sorts of garbage. Ramon sat in a deck chair, took a blunt out of his pocket, and lit it.

"That dude Sean, holmes, he's fuckin' dirty as dirt."

"Let's see it."

He pulled his cell phone from his pocket and opened a

video. Jen watched it over his shoulder, the sweet but pungent odor of the blunt wafting up to her.

The video had been shot on a cell phone and from a lower angle, as though someone held it at waist height. A group of men were standing around with Detective Henry Sean in the center, in plain clothes and sipping a beer. He was laughing and joking with the other men outside a bar.

One of the men took out a vial and tipped some white powder from it onto the back of his hand. He snorted it and then offered the vial to Sean.

The detective put some on his hand, snorted it, and then took the remnants on his finger and rubbed it on his gums.

"Yo," someone said, "there he is."

A car came to a stop next to them, and a large man stepped out. He was enormously muscular, his arms bulging inside his sleeves. He handed Sean a brown sack. Sean looked inside, rolled up the sack as tightly as he could, and tucked it into his pocket.

"H, dawg," the big man said, "as much as I'm payin' you, maybe you should be runnin' this shit."

The detective laughed.

The video went on with another snort of cocaine and a promise of prostitutes later at someone's house before it turned off. In total, it was thirty-eight seconds.

"How did you get this?" Jen asked.

"I know the big man was there, the one recording."

"You know if I use this, that detective will be fired. Your boy won't have him anymore."

"Shit, that big man, that fool's a punk. And this pig helpin' him, he ain't helpin' me. I ain't give a shit about him."

Jen stood up. She'd seen corruption up close with her time in the LAPD, but every time she saw it again, it made her blood boil. Those who were trusted by the public to protect them but who then went off and worked for the people they should have been arresting made her want to put on the badge again, join Internal Affairs, and hunt them down.

"How much?" she asked.

"For you? Two thousand."

"That video ain't worth two thousand."

He shrugged. "Ask your man."

She sighed and pulled out her phone and brought up Brigham in her contacts.

26

Brigham stood in front of Molly's condo door. Down the hall, it sounded like a party was going on. Music blared, muffled only slightly by the walls, and after a few moments a girl came stumbling out, giggling. She glanced over at Brigham and flicked her hair away from her eyes.

"'Sup, cutie," she slurred.

"Hi."

The girl was dragged back inside by another girl who appeared even more drunk, and the door closed. Brigham breathed in deeply, let it out through his nose, and then knocked on the door. Molly opened it, wearing her UCLA sweatshirt. She grinned and said, "Your phone must not be working."

"Must not be."

She opened the door and let him come in. He flopped on the couch nearest the windows overlooking the city. The sky was clear, no clouds, and the moonlight bathed the room in a dim glow.

"Do you know, moonlight doesn't actually exist," he said. "It's the sun's light reflecting off the moon. But it feels different. It feels like it's something different. Our senses can be completely wrong."

"But it doesn't make it any less beautiful, does it?"

He shook his head. "That's the scariest part—that we could be completely wrong and happy in our ignorance."

She sat next to him and lightly touched his shoulder. Her soft hand sent a small shock through him as her fingers moved up to his neck. They sat in silence a long time, so long that he felt himself drifting off to sleep. He forced himself awake by sitting up and leaning his elbows on his thighs.

"How's work?" he said.

She grinned. "Do you really want to know?"

"Yes, I really do."

"So far I've had about a thousand homeless people arrested for things that shouldn't really be crimes. I appeared in court once, prosecuting a drug dealer for stealing the money of another drug dealer. Oh, and I inherited a case of a domestic violence victim who didn't show up to court to testify against her scumbag husband, so my direct boss is making me arrest and prosecute her for failing to appear on a court order."

"Sounds fun."

"It is," she said, her tone making it clear that that was exactly what it wasn't. She curled her legs up under her.

"No one's forcing you to stay there."

"I don't know. Maybe I jumped the gun, but I want to give it some time."

Brigham felt sleep coming over him as if someone were pouring warm water over his head and he was slipping into a bath. Her condo always had that effect on him. Soft New Age music played through speakers that must've been in the walls. She got cold easily, so she kept the temperature above normal.

"Stay the night with me," she said.

He nodded, and as he leaned in to kiss her, his cell phone vibrated in his pocket. She must've felt it, too, because she smiled and rested her forehead against his. He took the phone out and saw that it was Jen.

"Hey," he said. "Kind of a bad time."

"If that was true, you wouldn't have answered."

"I hate how smart you are. What did you need?"

"The Ted Montgomery case. There's something you need to see. Something we're gonna have to pay for. But I want you to see it first."

"What?"

"I think it's best you see it. And bring your checkbook."

As they got off the freeway, Brigham glanced over at Molly. She was the perfect beauty, nothing plastic or artificial. She looked alluring with or without makeup, and her confidence and fierce intelligence shone through like a beacon. One thing Brigham had noticed whenever he went out with her was that men didn't stare or hit on her as much as he thought they would.

He had been puzzled by it for a long time. There was a difference between sultry and slutty, and he wondered if men only responded to the slutty and not the sultry. It wasn't until months into their relationship that he figured out what it was: men didn't see it.

The powerful intellect, the confidence that required no one else's approval, the assertiveness and strength... most men couldn't see it. That wasn't what they looked for in women, and so when they came across it, they had no idea what it was.

Suddenly, with that one thought, Brigham pitied Molly. He could picture a lifetime of neglect and bullying by people who were her intellectual inferior, the whole time Molly questioning what was wrong with her when the problem actually lay with others.

"Maybe we shouldn't have driven a luxury car into West Valley in the middle of the night," he said.

"It's hardly the middle of the night. And I've got a gun in the glove box."

"Since when?"

"Since three days ago when I began prosecuting people."

They passed Valley Fair Mall, a run-down mall the city had recently renovated. It didn't appear any better off than before. Brigham looked at the list of movies playing at the mall's theater.

"You know, I haven't been to a movie in like three years," he said.

"Seriously?"

"Yeah."

"Well, how about this Friday?"

"I did kind of want to see the new Spiderman."

She chuckled. "Why aren't I surprised?"

The neighborhood they were in was typical for West Valley. The city's median income per household was almost thirty percent less than Salt Lake City's, just twenty miles away. It had the highest crime rate of any city in Utah and in fact had been found to be one of America's most dangerous cities according to the FBI crime data, along with its neighboring cities, Kearns and Magna. Together, they formed the most dangerous area in the Mountain West, with one violent or property crime occurring every five seconds.

They found the home they were looking for and parked out front. Brigham saw several men on the porch, and they eyed him as if he were a cop.

"Wait here," he said.

"No way. I'm not letting you go in there by yourself."

"Molly, this is about a case that your office is prosecuting. I can't let you see whatever my investigator has in there."

"Oh," she said. "I didn't even… Yeah, I'll wait here."

Brigham stepped out of the car and walked, as slowly and nonthreateningly as he could, to the front porch. "Hi," he said. "I'm looking for Jennifer Vest? She told me to meet her here."

One man, probably no older than twenty, blew out a puff of acrid smoke and said, "She in back."

"Thanks."

He snuck past them, careful not to step on anyone's shoes, and entered the house.

A party was in full swing. Kid Frost was blaring over a stereo, a song Brigham recognized from high school, and he tried to make his way to the back without touching anyone. A white guy in a suit at a Hispanic gang party was asking for an ass kicking.

He got to the back door and saw Jen and another man sitting in deck chairs smoking. He stopped next to her, and she smiled.

"Surprised you actually had the guts to come down. Most lawyers are scared of this place."

"I've seen worse. What did you have for me?"

"This is Ramon. Ramon, Brigham. Ted Montgomery's lawyer."

Ramon blew out a puff of smoke and held a cell phone up. "Check this out, holmes."

Brigham watched the video.

His guts tightened to the point that it was uncomfortable.

A mix of disgust and excitement coursed through him, and he didn't know whether to celebrate that the testimony of one of the State's key witnesses was blown or to be outraged that a cop who investigated a few hundred cases a year could be bought so easily.

"Friend of Ramon's is recording," Jen said. "But you'd have one problem; he won't come to court. I don't know how you'd get it in without someone there to vouch for it."

"I don't need anyone there if it's used to impeach a witness."

"I'm guessing you want it then?"

"Of course. Why wouldn't I?"

"Because it's two thousand dollars."

"That's fine. I'll pay it out of Ted's fee." He turned to Ramon. "Can you email it to me?"

"No problem."

"Um, this might be a weird question, but you okay taking a check? I don't have two grand in cash laying around."

"For you," Ramon said with a wide smile, "I won't even require ID."

27

Brigham watched Rebecca watching the video in their conference room. He'd already seen it more times than he could count, but the expression on her face was what he wanted to see. It would likely be the same expression the jury would have when they saw it.

Rebecca's mouth fell open as if she were on a sitcom. Brigham couldn't help but grin.

"Holy shit," she said. "I can't believe I just saw that. That guy's a homicide detective."

"They don't pay cops a lot. Robbery-Homicide as a detective is a little better, but if you've got a bunch of kids and a wife to support, that small paycheck really stings."

She shook her head and mumbled "Holy shit" again. "So what're we gonna do? Take it to the judge or something?"

"No, no way. I want to surprise the prosecution with this. I'm not handing it over, either."

"But they filed a reverse discovery motion. We have to give them anything we're gonna use in trial."

"I'm not going to use it in trial. I'm going to use it as impeachment."

"And we don't have to give notice for impeachment evidence. Nice."

"Not really. I would've rather presented it to the jury with someone vouching for it, but the guy who took the video refused to come to court."

She straightened her glasses. "So you're just gonna ask him if he's ever accepted bribes and then when he says no show this to impeach him?"

"Yup."

"What if he says yes?"

"If we had an honest cop who admitted all his mistakes, it'd be tough to make him look bad in front of the jury. In fact it might even backfire on us. But no way he says yes. No cop in the world would say yes to that question."

"Can't we just use it so he doesn't take the stand at all? I mean, the jury's gonna remember what he said, even if he is a crooked cop."

He shook his head. "Things like this go to weight, not admissibility, meaning the jury can weigh whether this is enough to disregard his testimony. Has nothing to do with whether his testimony is admissible, though."

She adjusted her glasses, looking down at the still image of the detective accepting a brown bag from a street thug. "Holy shit."

They spent several days analyzing the video: every detail, every sentence, every background noise. Brigham made a transcript of it and read the transcript a few times. This video was a good starting point, a wedge to pry open the door that would lead to a not-guilty verdict. But it wasn't enough. The fact was, even if the jury disregarded the testimony of the detective and Ted's admission of guilt in front of him, the nurse still saw the death. And there were the children.

Monica was old enough to be considered an adult, but Devan and David were too young to take the stand without prior approval of the judge, and no such approval had been asked for by the prosecution.

On Saturday, Brigham came to the office and stood in the lobby, wondering what had brought him in on the weekend. He tried to never come in on weekends if he could avoid it.

That uneasy feeling was still tightening his guts, and he couldn't wait for this case to be done with. It brought up things better left forgotten.

He went up to the office and saw Scotty milling around. He was humming to himself and organizing stacks of files.

"What're you doing here?" Brigham asked.

"Oh. Hey. Just catching up. You?" he said.

"Came to work on my crosses in Montgomery. I didn't know you ever came in on a Saturday."

He looked away sheepishly. "You've been so busy, I didn't want to give you any of the new cases we've been signing up."

Brigham leaned on the filing cabinets. "I'm not a one-trick pony. I can handle more. But thank you."

"You don't want to defend shoplifting and DUIs when you got something like this. When we lose thefts, I mean, who gives a shit? They'll have to take a class, but so what? They can get it expunged from their records in a few years. But losing the Montgomery thing… that guy will die inside, and his kids'll be without a father. That's a lot of pressure."

"You know, I read that criminal defense attorneys have the lowest life expectancies of any profession because of the stress."

Scotty grinned. "Tommy used to say it feels like your balls are always in a vise, and there's two ways to react to it: you can hate your balls, or you can love the vise. But if you hate the vise, then it's time to find another job."

He chuckled. "I sure could use some of his advice right about now." He paused. "You and I never talked about his death."

"Nope."

"Do you want to?"

"Do I want to what?"

"Talk about Tommy's death."

Scotty twitched, his shoulder going up and then relaxing.

"Not really. There's nothing to talk about. He had a lot of demons that followed him here. He knew it was coming. He never talked about the future without saying something like, 'If I make it to fifty,' stuff like that."

Brigham looked over the files Scotty was organizing. "Thanks, Scotty. For everything. I know you took a big chance coming out with a new lawyer who doesn't know anything."

"Shit," he said, returning to his files, "you know more than any attorney I know. You just don't recognize it."

Brigham worked late into the night, and when he left the office, the moon was out. He hadn't even noticed the transition from light to dark. It was disquieting for a few minutes to step out into the night when he expected the day.

He waited at the stop for the train. The blinking sign said it'd be eight minutes before the next train, so he sat down and stared at the passing cars. When he'd been a kid, he'd made up stories about the people he saw on the streets or at a mall. That guy was a spy, that guy was a bank robber and didn't want his wife to know, that gal was going to be an astronaut who walked on Mars... He was fascinated by people and their stories.

People were so fragile, so weak, and subject to so much pain that the overwhelming emotion he felt when he looked at them was pity. He saw people, and he just felt sorry for them.

They had to go through all this just to live.

The train pulled to a stop, and he hopped on. He sat on a bench at the back and stared out the windows as the train pulled away. The city passed before him as flashes of light. He still made up stories about the people he saw, but the stories were much harder to take in.

That guy was starving, that woman was prostituting herself to feed a son at home, that guy was planning a robbery to pay for his daughter's hospital bills. He wondered if the difference between childhood and adulthood was the recognition that the world wasn't divided into good and bad people—just good and bad decisions.

The Trax stopped near the pizzeria, and he stepped off and hurried up the sidewalk. He kept his hands in his pockets and his head down. The city was a sea of blinking lights behind him. The pizzeria stood on top of a small hill close to the University of Utah. He'd transferred there after Katrina destroyed his own law school. Everyone transferred to any schools that would take them, and most people searched out of state. The devastation made the city seem unrecognizable, and no one wanted to stay. Luckily, Brigham was done and had to take only a few Bar prep courses in Utah, so the change didn't shock him as it had some of his classmates who transferred to different states.

He went down the steps to the pizzeria. The walls were

coated with crayon, marker, or pen from every student who had come through here in the past fifty years. They wrote names, anagrams, aphorisms, and sometimes just ranted on every inch of the interior brick walls. The Pie was a staple of the University of Utah as much as any of the buildings on campus. The atmosphere was always jovial and the pizza hot and gooey, but that's not why Brigham came here.

Sitting in the corner, he could watch people for hours without anyone noticing: the way they spoke, the way they moved and interacted with one another. The way their eyes betrayed their true emotions when their words tried to convey something else. Jury selection wasn't about asking questions, it was about gut feelings. The half a second when he first saw someone and got an impression was the moment Brigham used to pick his jury. Everything else didn't work.

He ordered a slice of barbeque chicken and a Diet Coke and sat in his favorite corner seat. The place was packed and loud, The Doors blaring from the jukebox tucked away in the opposite corner. He scanned the crowd and was about to dig into his pizza when he saw a familiar face: Rebecca.

She was seated with three of her friends, splitting a large pizza and a pitcher of beer. He watched her, the way she laughed carelessly and freely. She had a joy that Molly lacked. Molly was somber and slightly melancholy, where Rebecca seemed to live in wonder of the things around her. He could see that if he hadn't been with Molly…

But there was no use thinking of things like that. He was with her, and he cared deeply for her even if the cold sting of betrayal still stuck in his guts like an ice pick.

Rebecca saw him, said something to her friends, and came over.

"Hey," she said, a wide smile on her face.

"Hey."

She sat down. "I didn't know you came here."

"I took some classes at the U before the Bar. I'd come here all the time. Best pizza I've ever had."

She hesitated. "Are you here alone?"

"Yeah."

"Why don't you come join us?"

"And ruin your girls' night? I'm cool."

"You're not going to ruin it. Come hang with us."

"I'm okay. I gotta get home and work after this anyway."

She pulled her shirtsleeves over her fingers and wrists, absently playing with them a moment. "Hold on."

She rose and walked to her friends and said something to them that didn't make them happy. They discussed it a moment, though Brigham couldn't hear a word they were saying, and then Rebecca came back and sat across from him.

"What was that?" he asked.

"I told them I had to bail for work. Now we can both

work at your house."

"It's fine, be with your friends. I'm really okay."

She hesitated. "I'd rather be with you."

Brigham swallowed and looked away. "I don't think that's a good idea."

"Why not?"

"Because I'm with Molly."

"Are you? Because it seems like you're here by yourself."

The truth stung. Since she'd gone to the DA's office, something was different between the two of them, some secret that they both knew about but neither one of them wanted to discuss. But he wasn't sure what that secret was.

"I better go." He rose from the table, leaving his food, and slipped past her and out of the restaurant. As he headed up the stairs, he glanced inside and saw her return to her table, her eyes on him until he reached the top and couldn't see her anymore.

28

It'd been three days since Brigham had seen Molly. They'd texted several times and spoken on the phone once, but he could tell something had changed, and they both knew it. For him, it wasn't that she worked for Vince Dale, although he was one of the worst people Brigham knew, a man who used power because he could. When he'd run for office, he'd campaigned to abolish the distinction between juvenile and adult crime. "If a kid commits an adult crime, he should face an adult punishment," he had said.

It was a statement the hard-line voters of his district couldn't get enough of. It ignored all the research and common sense that said children were not adults, that they could not think like adults, could not reason like adults and determine consequences. But it was catchy and made him appear tough on crime. Now he was working on a new child-crimes task force at the DA's office that was to begin trying more juveniles as adults.

Brigham knew Vince didn't really care one way or the other about whether juveniles were tried as adults. It was a maneuver to get into office. And once there, he couldn't even imagine how hard and dirty Vince Dale would fight to keep his post as top prosecutor.

Brigham had finished preparing his cross-examinations of the State's witnesses in Ted's case. The preparation was nothing more than going through various scenarios and general ideas about what he would attack should that scenario present itself. The fact was, no one ever really knew what a witness was going to say on the stand, and much of the cross would be based on what was brought out on direct examination by the prosecutor.

The trial was coming up, and Ted hadn't come in for any preparation. Brigham had left half a dozen messages and sent email, but Ted hadn't responded. In desperation, Brigham called his brother Timothy, who one of his paralegals had wisely collected contact information from.

"This is Tim," he said.

"Tim, hey, it's Brigham Theodore, Ted's lawyer. Have you seen him? I can't get him to return my calls."

"Yeah, I saw him yesterday. He's been spending a bunch of time with his kids."

Brigham leaned back and put his feet on his desk, staring up at the wooden slats in the ceiling. "I really need him to come to my office to go over his testimony. I've called several times. And texted and emailed."

"Well, I'll try and let him know you're lookin' for him."

"Okay. Thanks. So how long are you in Utah for?"

"Until this whole shit-storm blows over. Depending on

which way it goes, I might be inheriting three kids."

"You're a saint for it."

"I love the kiddos. What else can I do?"

"Yeah… well, if you see him, please tell him to call me."

"Will do."

Brigham hung up and let his head rest on the back of his chair. It wasn't uncommon for clients to disregard the advice of their lawyers. In fact, it was more the norm, and the aberration was following the advice. But on a murder case in which he had three children to think of, Brigham thought Ted should take it a little more seriously. It was almost as if he wanted to be convicted.

As the day drew to a close, he realized he'd made no progress since the day had begun. He'd thought about the trial all day, worked on different aspects of it for eight hours straight, and felt absolutely no more prepared, running in place and not moving forward an inch.

Night fell quickly. Tomorrow, he decided, he wouldn't be at the office. Scotty was doing a great job training Rebecca and Gerald, and Brigham didn't have any court time scheduled until after the Montgomery trial. To get a fresh perspective, maybe he needed to go down to the canyons tomorrow or go camping. Something to change the environment and hopefully get some new inspiration.

As he was heading out of the office, the elevator dinged

and opened. Molly stepped out wearing a black suit with a red blouse. Brigham's heart dropped into his stomach. The pain told him he had missed her, though his mind told him he was still angry with her.

"Hi," he said.

She grinned. "Hi." She walked down the hallway, glancing into the floor-to-ceiling windows that made up the front wall of the law firm. "Never thought I'd feel weird coming here. It felt like home."

"It was your home. It still is."

She sighed and leaned against the wall. "How's everyone?"

"Good. Lexi's pregnant. They're really psyched."

"That's fantastic! They've been trying for three years."

"Yeah, she was bouncing off the walls today." He moved next to her and leaned against the wall as well, catching a glimpse of their reflection in the glass. "How's protecting the public going?"

"I'm not sure who I'm protecting anymore. Half of what we do seems to be covering our asses so our supervisor doesn't ream us. But I had a case today where a victim of domestic violence didn't have anywhere to go. I set her up with the YWCA and she got a place to stay for her and her kids. She started crying in my office and gave me a hug."

"That had to feel good."

"Yeah, it did. I didn't think… for a long time, I thought

the law was just about billing hours on some anonymous case. I didn't realize there was humanity in everything we did. Someone's affected by whatever we do."

Brigham took out a roll of Life Savers and popped one in his mouth. He offered them to Molly, and she skipped the top green one and got the next one, which was red. "I'm going away for a day," he told her. "Maybe Moab or somewhere. Come with me."

"There's nothing in the world I would love to do more, but I can't just leave anymore. I just started. How would that look?"

"Not good, I bet."

"I'm on a team, and so when one of us slacks off, everyone else has to make up the work. It's not fair to my team to do that to them."

"Can we do something this weekend?"

"I have a trial coming up, actually. I was going to go in Saturday and prep it."

Brigham didn't say anything for a long enough time that the only thing that broke the silence was the cleaning crew coming up the elevators and shyly filing past them into the office.

"Is this it?" Brigham said. "Is this our life now? Trying to fit in time when we can see each other?"

"I think that's what couples do."

"I wouldn't know. I've never been part of a couple. I mean, I had girlfriends in high school and stuff, but nothing serious. Not until… this. I don't know how it works."

She turned to face him, taking his hands in hers. They were soft and sent chills up his back. "It works the way every relationship works. We grow together. Two lives being shared together. We might be taking different paths, but we're going in the same direction. You have to remember that."

He leaned in and kissed her. Their lips locked, and he could taste her fruity lip balm. He pulled away and rested his forehead against hers, staring at her shoes.

"Red pumps, huh?"

"They're absolutely killing my feet. I think I'm gonna try to get away with sweats and sneakers from now on."

"Your mom was wearing sweats when I met her the first time. She still looked hot."

She playfully punched him in the chest. "Scumbag."

"What? It's not scummy to call a beautiful woman beautiful."

"Ew, Brigham, stop it."

He chuckled. "Well, you can't go away with me and you can't spend the weekend with me. How about a late dinner?"

"I'd love that."

He took her hand, and they left the building.

29

Almost two weeks into her new job, Molly felt the ease of familiarity coming into her daily routine. She arrived at work and checked her email then her calendar for that day and pulled the cases that had been added the night before. The DA's office had seventy-four trial prosecutors, and people called in sick or late or had some other reason they couldn't make it to court on time. Their cases were shuffled around and spread among the prosecutors who were there.

She found an afternoon felony calendar that hadn't been there the night before. There were fifty to sixty felony cases, and she was expected to have read the police reports on each and negotiate with the defense attorneys. She emailed her paralegal to pull the cases for that calendar and stack them on her desk.

Her calendar dinged. It was time for a team meeting. She rose and followed the line of attorneys on her floor to the conference room for the special prosecutions division.

Every prosecutor, no matter their division, had to cover calendars when needed and even did things as mundane as take public complaints for investigation. Molly had been assigned that shift once and quickly found it was just people who had already gone to the police and either weren't taken seriously or felt the police weren't moving quickly enough. Half the public complaints she'd heard were about neighbors encroaching on property or being too loud.

The conference room was filled with the attorneys and staff of the SP division. Molly found a chair against the wall and sat down, crossing her legs and noticing a run in her pantyhose. It was thin, barely noticeable, but now that she'd seen it, she couldn't focus on anything else. She crossed her legs the other way and hoped no one noticed.

Molly thought the team leader of the SP division, Johnny Presto, had a ridiculous name for such a serious position. Johnny scanned a document on his tablet every meeting and then began doling out assignments. He went around the room, and each attorney got something new, mostly cases that had appeared on the news. There was one politician, someone in the legislature who had urinated on a prostitute, and the prostitute then alleged that he raped her when she objected. It was a tough case from the get-go, considering the victim was a prostitute and in the legislator's hotel room willingly. Still, it sounded like an interesting case, and Molly wished she'd gotten it.

When Johnny came to her, he looked at his tablet and said, "Molly, you got the Ted Montgomery case as second chair.

You'll be helping Debra on it." He moved on to the next person. "Jessica, I want you to—"

"Wait a second," Molly interrupted. "Ted Montgomery? The man who killed his wife when she was dying of cancer?"

"Yeah," Johnny said.

"I can't do that. I was at the firm that's defending him. That's a clear conflict. I can't go anywhere near that case."

"Oh, well, sorry, but that's how it is. Comes from the big man himself."

Molly felt anger rise in her belly. "Vince assigned me to that case?"

"Yeah. Received the email this morning."

Molly stormed out of the meeting. Johnny said something behind her, but she didn't stop. She marched to the elevators and hit the button for the floor above. Rage seethed in her, and she had to pace the elevator to keep from going crazy as it slowly rose.

She got off on that floor and scanned her ID on the locked glass door. She was waved past the metal detectors and stormed her way to Vince's office. She opened the door as his secretary said something about making an appointment.

She had wanted to be calm and sit down and discuss everything with him. Maybe he'd had a good reason to do what he did. When she saw his face as he was speaking with an Asian man seated across from him, all that went out the window.

"You son of a bitch."

"Good morning to you, too," he said without missing a beat. He looked at the man. "Better excuse us, Thomas."

The man, who Molly had never seen before, got up and left. Molly stood across from him, her arms folded as she paced in front of the desk.

"You son of a bitch," she mumbled.

"Already said that."

"Don't be a smug prick. I can't believe I actually thought you'd tell the truth." She planted herself a few feet away from him. "You value me and want me at the office," she said sarcastically. "I'm an excellent attorney."

"You are."

"Bullshit! You brought me over just so you could put me on the Montgomery case. You're so scared of losing to Brigham again that you went through this whole thing just to mess with his head."

"That's true."

She took a step back, shaking her head. "Brigham was right about you. Power is all you care about. Him beating this office on another high-profile case is a ding on your power. You used me."

He exhaled. "Molly, I do think you're an excellent attorney. And I did want you here. I realized your firm was on the Montgomery case after I'd already hired you."

"I don't believe you."

"Believe what you want. It's the truth."

She paced around the desk. "It's a conflict. I couldn't appear on it if I wanted to, and I don't."

"Do you know the details of the case? Did you ever talk to Ted Montgomery? Ever even read the discovery we sent?"

She hesitated. "No, but that doesn't matter. I was an attorney at the firm defending him."

"The ethical rules on conflicts are murky at best. I think we can get Judge Lawrence to agree with us."

"No way she will."

"She will. Watch."

"He's my boyfriend, Vince. How do you expect me to go up against him?"

"I expect you to be a professional who works at an office that protects the public. As a professional, you will have to do things you don't enjoy. That's life. If you don't like it, no one's forcing you to stay."

She approached the desk and placed her hands on it, leaning close to him. "There's a line, Vince. You don't see it until you cross it, but there's a line. If you're hurting the public in order to protect them, then you're their greatest threat. Not some mugger or car thief."

He rose, a flash of anger on his face that made his lips go straight as cardboard. "Get the hell outta my office and go do your job."

Molly turned and stormed out, slamming the door behind her.

30

The night before the trial, Brigham lay in his bed, staring at the ceiling. The light from the moon was coming through the blinds and lighting up the room. He reached over and opened the blinds to get a better view. The moon was full without any clouds in the sky. He put his hands behind his head and stared at it a long while, then hopped out of bed and threw on some sneakers and a tracksuit.

He ran out of the house and grabbed his bike, which he took to the Trax station. No one else was out this late at night, and he sat at the stop by himself, staring at the blinking lights of a bank marquee across the street. The sleep deprivation wouldn't bother him: he never slept the night before a trial.

The train was empty when it arrived, and he chose to stand rather than sit. The stop he wanted was about three miles away, and he hopped off, rode his bike through the residential neighborhood, and found the house he was looking for.

All the lights were off in Ted's home. Brigham didn't even know if he was actually there. He hadn't had any contact with him for a few days other than a quick email confirming the date and time of the trial. No preparation had gone into his testimony, and Ted had no idea what was going to be asked of him on cross-examination. He would be going into the trial even more blind than Brigham.

Brigham knocked softly, and then he knocked again. Not wanting to wake the kids, he got a pebble and scanned the house. A room on the main floor had the windows open, and he could see diagrams on the wall and the headboard of a bed. He pegged the side of the house with the pebble, and then did it again with another one.

Someone stirred and then rose. Ted's frame came into view as he stared at Brigham.

"Brigham?" he whispered.

"Open the door. We need to talk, right now."

"Now? It's, like, one in the morning."

"*Now*, Ted."

"Okay, hang on."

Ted seemed to take his time getting to the front door and stepped out onto the porch in his bathrobe and shut the door behind him. "What's going on?"

Brigham took a step toward him so he was only inches from his face. "What the hell's the matter with you?"

"What? What do you—"

"Ted," he said angrily, "what the hell's the matter with you? Huh? You asked me to help you, paid me a small fortune, and then won't even return my calls." Ted took a step away, and Brigham closed the distance again. "You wanna go to prison for the rest of your life? Is that what this is? Some sort of pseudo-suicide? To make up for what you did to your wife?"

"How dare you! I died that day with her. You don't know what that's like."

"The hell I don't," Brigham snapped. He turned away, staring at the front lawn. "I don't want to represent you anymore. As soon as the court opens, I'm going to strike the trial and tell the judge that I need to withdraw from the case."

Ted hesitated and then took a step toward him. "Don't do that," he said gently. "Please, don't do that."

"Then why aren't you helping me?" he said, turning around to face him.

Ted's shoulders slumped, and he gazed at the ground before collapsing onto one of the chairs set out on the porch. "I miss her every day, Brigham. At night, I still think she's here. I'll reach over to feel for her, but there's nothing there. Sometimes I wake up excited to see her, and the horror of what happened comes back to me. And I remember it all. It's like having to go through it again every single damn day. And I don't know if it's going to last the rest of my life or not. I'm scared. I'm scared of this trial, I'm scared of going to prison, I'm scared that I'll never see her again. I just wanted... I just wanted to be with my kids. Every second of every day that I could. I wanted to be with my kids."

Brigham sat in a chair next to him. "I can't do this alone. If you want me to stay on the case, it's truth time."

Ted looked at him. "You want to know where I got the morphine, don't you?"

"Yes."

Ted swallowed and looked away. He closed his eyes and mumbled something that sounded like *forgive me*. "This stays between us. I do not want you to use this in my defense, and as your client I forbid you to reveal it to anybody."

"You have my word."

He nodded. "I… I didn't kill my wife, Brigham. My brother did."

A breeze was blowing, and a house across the street had wind chimes. The sound was soothing but oddly creepy. Every horror movie Brigham could remember right now had wind chimes as the monster or killer stalked a neighborhood.

His mind went back to when he was young and he and his friend Andy would rent horror movies from a video store near their home. They could watch three slasher movies in a row and not get bored, though the movies were practically all the same.

Ted was gazing off into the distance, and neither of them spoke.

"What do you mean your brother killed her?"

"I mean, he killed her. It was something he and I had discussed. After Ruby and I discussed it, I needed someone to talk to, so I called him. He thought it was a good idea. Managed death is legal in Oregon, so I should transfer her to a hospital up there. But she was in so much pain they wouldn't let her leave. And I thought that Huntsman Cancer at the university was the best place in the world to treat it. If there was even a chance that she would..." He trailed off, his eyes glazing over. "But there wasn't. So my brother came down to stay with us. He worked with some shady pharmacist in Oregon to get the morphine—someone he met at the gym offering to sell steroids or something." Ted spread his hands. "I didn't even know about it."

"How did he do it?"

"He called me from the hospital and said that the kids and I needed to come down and say goodbye. That he was injecting her soon and she'd have about thirty minutes. I begged him not to. I cried, I pleaded," he said sadly. "I even tried to bribe him. But he said he was doing what I was too weak to do. And he was right. Tim's always been the stronger one. The quarterback of our high school football team, when I was in the chess club. He always had the hottest dates for dances while I took whoever he could set me up with. He was the alpha, and I think he always wanted to protect me. He just thought he was protecting me. He's not a bad person. He thought this was what I wanted."

"Was it?"

He shook his head. "No. I wanted as much time with her as possible, but I know now that was selfish. What happened was the right thing. My time with her was cut short, but she left in peace and love. It was a great gift to her, and I was too weak to do it." He put his face in his hands. "I was too damn weak to give it to her, and Tim had to do it."

"How did the hospital staff not see him?"

"I told him to leave. He did it for me and for my children, and for my wife. He did something that he knew was right, and that I didn't have the stomach to do. I didn't want him to pay for that. I forced him out of the hospital room and told him to go back to Oregon. I said I would deal with the fallout. He's wanted to come forward since I got charged, but I won't let him."

Brigham sat there a moment. "Ted," he said quietly, "we need to talk to the prosecutor about this."

"What? No. Absolutely not."

"You're looking at a life sentence for something you didn't do. We need to talk to the prosecutor."

"No. I won't do that to Tim. He's my kid brother. He's got his first child on the way, his entire life's ahead of him. I won't do that to him. You promised me you wouldn't say anything."

Brigham placed his elbows on his thighs and leaned forward, staring at the way the moonlight danced through the trees and cast shadows on the porch. "I won't tell anyone. But you have to convince your brother to come forward."

"No, I don't want him to. That's why I rushed the trial. He's devastated that I'm going through this, and he called me, crying, before they came down here. Said he was going to confess to everything. So I just want this over and done with before he gets the chance. He did me a favor I will never forget. And I'm doing the same thing for him now."

Brigham shook his head. "I can't do this. I can't watch you get convicted."

Ted, a melancholy smile on his face, said, "Yes, you can. Because you're all I've got left."

He went inside, leaving Brigham alone in the darkness of the porch.

31

When Brigham woke for the trial, he checked the clock and saw he'd gotten only about two hours of sleep. But he felt wired and energetic, a result, he guessed, from the adrenaline and anxiety coursing through him.

He had several voicemails from Molly, but he didn't check them. Not now.

A few days before, he'd been fitted for a proper suit, as his accountant had recommended. The suit fit so well that it almost made him uncomfortable, as if he were showing off. He hoped the jury wouldn't see it that way. To counteract this, he retrieved a watch from his dresser drawer: a Donald Duck watch, a present from his nephew when he'd gotten into law school. He made sure the watch was visible from all angles and then slipped on his shoes and headed out the door.

The bike ride to the courthouse took only ten minutes in light traffic. The sun wasn't fully out yet, and the sky was that odd color of orange between darkness and light. As he got to the courthouse steps and locked up his bike, he stared at the sky for a few seconds and couldn't move.

This was madness. Rushing the trial as they had, essentially, they were throwing witnesses up there and seeing what was going to come out of their mouths. He had no idea what was going to happen. But one good thing, he thought, was that the prosecutor didn't know either.

What choice did he have? He could either withdraw or respect his client's wishes. And he didn't want to withdraw—not now that he knew his client hadn't done it.

He went through the metal detectors, and his shoes made the scanners go off. He was asked to step aside, and was wanded.

He took the elevator up to Judge Lawrence's floor, who had inherited the case since she didn't actually do the preliminary hearing. The elevator was packed, but he couldn't understand anybody's conversations. It was like background noise. Everything was in slow motion.

Innocence or guilt wasn't really something he had ever considered. Brigham had looked only at what was fair and wanted that outcome for his clients. Looking back over the past year, he could think of only perhaps two or three clients that he felt were truly innocent and being unfairly prosecuted. Two or three out of five or six hundred. Those cases were for minor offenses, though. Shoplifting, pot possession… things that wouldn't haunt them for the rest of their lives.

Ted Montgomery would die in prison if Brigham lost this trial. An innocent man, confused and frightened, covering for his brother. Possibly.

Brigham wanted to believe everything his clients told him but had been burned too many times. In most cases, they were people with long criminal histories who had spent a lifetime lying to protect themselves and didn't understand when someone was truly there to help them. They lied to their own lawyers as much as to the police and prosecution.

Brigham wasn't certain if Ted was telling the truth, but there was an easy way to find out.

The courtroom wasn't open yet, but Ted was already there, along with his three children, Tim, and his wife.

"Tim, can I talk to you for a second?" Brigham said.

Ted's face dropped. Brigham knew he didn't want it discussed with Tim, so he would have to be careful.

Brigham opened a door to a small room marked Attorney/Client and waited for Tim to enter. Ted stood up and was about to say something but Brigham cut him off and said, "One minute."

Brigham sat across from Tim and just held his gaze. Tim was larger than Ted and had more gray hair, though he was the younger brother. He clearly lifted weights, and his muscles bulged under the polo shirt he was wearing. His eyes were a steel gray, and for a long time, the two men simply stared at each other.

"Did you?" Brigham asked.

Tim looked down. He folded his hands on the table, his

fingers interlacing. "He told you?" he asked softly.

"Tim, he's going to go to prison for the rest of his life. How can you sit by and let that happen?"

"You think I want to? I've tried to go to the police, like, ten times. Ted kept saying he would deny it and say I'm just covering for him. He'd get really pissed about it. The one thing he asked is that I watch the kids while he's gone. I love those kids; I'd do it anyway."

"How noble of you."

"Hey, this isn't easy for anybody. I loved Ruby. She was like my sister. I stuck a damn needle in her arm, and she was dead after that. That shit haunts me every night." He leaned back in the chair and released a big breath. "What can I do to help him?"

"You can take the stand, and tell the jury what you did."

"Ted wouldn't take that. He'd just get up there and contradict it."

"Not if he testifies first."

Tim held his gaze. "You're his lawyer. You know you're going against his wishes, right?"

"He can be pissed with me all he wants later. At least he'll be outta prison."

The word "prison" sent a small tremor through Timothy's face. His eyes widened and his lips parted slightly as he realized what testifying would mean.

"They're going to come after me hard, aren't they?"

"Maybe. But they might be so embarrassed that they had the wrong person they might give you a deal just to get this case outta the news."

"What kinda deal?"

"I don't know. But if Ted is acquitted, I will represent you for free. It would make Ted a former client with no repercussions available, since jeopardy would attach and they couldn't try him again. Which means I can use any information I want to defend you."

He shook his head. "How the hell did it come to this?"

"Why did you do it? If you could've gotten her to Oregon, euthanasia's legal there."

"I know. We tried. Her doctors and the hospital said it was a liability issue, and they couldn't release her. I think they just didn't want her to die, had some moral thing against it. And she didn't want to go until the very end. But by then she was in so much pain the doctors didn't believe her. They thought she was delusional from the pain."

Brigham leaned forward. "Help me, Tim. Help me save your brother's life. Testify for him."

He nodded. "I'll do it... I'll do it."

32

Brigham stepped out of the Attorney/Client room and saw Ted glaring at him. Brigham brushed past him and into the courtroom. If Ted asked him what was happening, he'd have to tell him. And Ted would ruin it during his testimony. The trial just had to start as quickly as possible so Ted could be distracted.

Brigham wasn't entirely sure about what he'd just done. He'd purposely disobeyed the wishes of his client. But he felt his duty was more than just doing what his clients wanted. His job was to look after them, and sometimes that meant doing the opposite of what they wanted if it was good for them in the long term.

He felt sorry for Timothy, too. With a baby on the way, he would likely be in prison for the baby's birth, unable to see his child grow up. But Brigham felt he could create enough of a stir in the media about the DA's office having arrested and put on trial an innocent man that he could push them into giving Tim a good deal. Maybe even avoiding prison altogether and just serving a few months in the county jail.

But Timothy was not his client right now. Ted was.

The courtroom was cold, though there were no windows or open doors. He walked to the defense table and saw Debra setting up some poster-board presentations. The homicide statute was most prominent, as was diminished capacity and a discussion of how the burden of proof shifted to the defense for diminished capacity: the defense actually had to present evidence for it, and the State was not required to provide any to the contrary. Brigham was required to provide proof of their affirmative defense before trial, but he wished that wasn't the law. It seemed unfair that a man fighting for his life had to tell the prosecution beforehand how he was going to defend himself.

Brigham sat at the defense table and rested his hand on it. It felt cool.

What he was about to do would be considered unethical. He was disobeying a direct request by the client not to reveal information learned through confidential communications. Ted, if he filed a Bar complaint, could get Brigham suspended, maybe even disbarred if the Utah State Bar felt the violation was egregious enough.

The weight of it made him anxious, but the weight of losing this trial and watching an innocent man with three children die in prison was heavier. He would do it and deal with the repercussions as they came.

Debra crossed the courtroom and stood next to him with

her arms folded. "Want to talk?"

"Is there a point?"

"Same offer as before."

"Then no, we don't need to talk."

She shrugged and went back to her table.

Brigham heard the double doors leading into the courtroom open. He glanced back to see who it was and saw Molly walking into the courtroom. She smiled slightly at him and then sat at the prosecution table. He stared at her, not believing what he was seeing. She mouthed the words, "I'm sorry."

Brigham was on his feet. "What the hell is this?"

"What?" Debra said. "She's second-chairing."

"What are you talking about? She was a partner at the firm that's defending him. She can't do that."

"Take it up with the judge."

Brigham looked at Molly. "Really? You're good with this?"

"I objected to it. But I was ordered to come down and do the trial."

"Ordered? What are you, cannon fodder? Fuck Vince Dale. Quit."

"Brigham," she said, "calm down."

"Calm down? He's got my girlfriend going up against me, my girlfriend who heard me talk about this case, and I'm supposed to be calm. He's doing this to screw with me, Molly.

How could you go along with it?"

"I've got a job to do and so do you. We don't need to make this personal. And by the way, answer your phone. I tried calling you a dozen times to tell you."

Brigham shook his head. "I don't believe this."

He sat back down at the defense table, unable to look at her. Losing his temper wasn't something he did often, and he didn't quite know how to handle it. All the emotions were boiling up inside him and growing louder, and he didn't know how to get them out. He rose and stormed out of the courtroom, brushing past Ted and his family.

Outside the courtroom, he found an empty Attorney/Client room. Locking the door, he paced around the room, and then seemingly with a burst of energy he didn't know was coming, he flipped over the table. A loud crash echoed in the small room and he shouted, "Shit."

He covered his face in his hands and took a deep breath. Then he leaned against the wall and slid down to the floor. Not only could he be disbarred over this case, he was pretty certain his relationship of one year had just ended.

His head dipped low, against his arms, and he closed his eyes. There was only one person in the world he felt like calling right now, and it made him feel like a child that he wanted to do it. But he pulled out his phone and dialed the number anyway.

"Brigham, oh my gosh, how are you?"

"Hey, Ma. I'm okay. I just wanted to call and say hi." He leaned his head back against the wall. "How's everybody there?"

"Good. Same as always. You remember Candice Robbins? From church? You two used to play together and you said you would get married when you got older."

"Yeah, I remember her."

"Well, she got married. It's a banker from Wall Street. She's moving to Manhattan. Can you believe that? Little Candice Robbins in Manhattan."

He took in a deep breath and stretched his legs out. "I miss your food. I could really use your bourbon chicken."

"Well, anytime you want to, you come out here."

"Yeah, I'll try to make it this summer… Listen, I gotta run to court. I just wanted to check up on you really quick."

"Aren't you sweet, but I'm your mother."

"What does that mean?"

"It means I knew you felt crummy the moment you spoke. What's the matter, baby?"

He grinned. She had always had the eerie ability that mothers had to see through any façade he built. "Just work trouble. Nothing serious."

"Okay, well, if you need to talk to anybody, I'm here for you."

"Thanks, Ma. I'll call you soon."

He slipped the phone into his pocket and stood up. He was glad nobody had come in to check when he'd tipped the table over. He straightened it and checked to make sure there wasn't any damage. When he was convinced everything was how he'd found it, he left the room and went back to the defense table. The judge would be coming out soon.

33

The bailiff called for everyone to rise. Brigham did so, buttoning the top button on his suit coat. He glanced behind him and saw Ted's family in the audience, surrounded by the media: several reporters from websites and blogs that followed the world of crime, as well as two cameras. Sitting next to him at the defense table was Ted, and on Ted's other side was Rebecca.

The judge took the bench and adjusted the files on her desk before turning on her computer. She then glanced at both parties and said, "You may be seated." When the lawyers sat, she said, "Any issues before we bring out the jury panel?"

"May I approach?" Brigham asked.

"Certainly."

Brigham rose and went to the judge's bench. "Your Honor, the State has asked Ms. Molly Becker to second-chair this trial. Ms. Becker is a former partner at my firm. She was with my firm when Mr. Montgomery hired us. It's a clear conflict, and I'm worried she has confidential information obtained by privileged communications that will be used against my client. I would ask the Court to remove the Salt Lake County District Attorney's Office due to a conflict and the violation of attorney–client privilege."

"Ms. Flynn, what's going on?"

"Your Honor, the ethical rules allow for this situation as long as the party involved has no confidential information about the client. And even then, the rules allow the agency to continue on the case as long as the interested party was walled off from any involvement in the case previously. Ms. Becker has no confidential information whatsoever. Mr. Montgomery was Mr. Theodore's client and has never said a word to Ms. Becker. Further, she knew nothing about the case other than that her firm was representing him."

The judge thought a moment and said, "Well, my question is, why am I hearing about this now?"

Brigham replied, "I literally found out as she walked into the courtroom, Your Honor."

The judge said, "Let me look at the rules, hold on."

She turned to her computer and was on it a good ten minutes. The silence in the courtroom was palpable. Most people thought judges knew the law and ethics rules off the tops of their heads, but that just wasn't true. Nobody knew. There was no reason to when all the codes, ordinances, and ethical rules could be kept on a smartphone.

Brigham couldn't bring himself to look over at Ted, much less at Molly. He kept his eyes on the wooden bench surrounding the judge in front of him. Someone had carved the words "Fight the power" into it with a pen.

"Under Rule 1.8 K, it states that, 'While lawyers are associated in a firm, a prohibition in the foregoing paragraphs A through I that applies to one of them shall apply to all of them.' And in the preceding paragraph section B, it states that 'a lawyer shall not use any information gained in the representation of a client to the client's disadvantage in further proceedings.' So basically, a lawyer can't use confidential information to harm their client, and if a lawyer from one firm represents a client, these rules apply to all the lawyers in the firm. That was my previous understanding of the rules, as well."

Debra said, "But the key to that is that we can't use any information detrimental to the client that was gained during the representation. There was no information gained during the representation other than his name and a general description of the case, which was public information anyway. Ms. Becker literally doesn't have anything to hurt the defendant with."

"Your Honor," Brigham said, "these rules are not meant to be bent when it suits the Court. It is a per se conflict, regardless of the amount of information or its quality. And the fact is, we don't know what's important right now. What if something that Ms. Becker overheard by the water cooler is pivotal in the trial?"

The judge leaned back, thought a moment, and then said,

"It's going too far. I'm not going to allow it. Ms. Flynn, the conflict is clear, and Mr. Theodore is right; we don't know what she knows until something pops up. You can either go forward with another second chair, or I will grant Mr. Theodore's request that the Salt Lake County District Attorney's Office be disqualified from the prosecution of Ted Montgomery."

Debra was going to say something but sighed instead and said, "We will be going forward without her."

"Very well, then. Anything further from either party?"

"No, Your Honor."

"No, Your Honor."

"Great. Then let's bring out the panel."

Jury selection was the least interesting part of any trial for Brigham. Hundreds of millions of dollars a year were spent on jury-selection experts, and all the valid research that had been performed on them said that there was no correlation between money spent on experts and favorable jury outcomes. Human beings were too complex and too deceptive for anyone to ever truly know how they were going to rule on a particular case.

The judge explained the criminal process to the jury pool and that, in Utah, noncapital felonies had eight jurors along with two alternates in case any of the eight became sick or had to leave for some other reason. Brigham wasn't really paying attention. He was focused on how to get Timothy

Montgomery's testimony in.

Technically, he was supposed to give ten days' notice to the prosecution of any witnesses he intended to call to trial, or reasonable notice if that wasn't possible. He wanted to surprise the prosecution with Tim as much as possible, so there was only one way to do that.

The jury pool was asked a series of questions by the judge: Have you ever been convicted of a felony? Are you or any members of your family in law enforcement? Do you feel you can be impartial in a criminal trial?

The questions were nonsense. Everyone felt they were objective, rational people that could be fair. No one could admit that they were ruled by forces they couldn't even see, much less understand and acknowledge. Every person in the pool had things they were hiding from the world, things that would influence how they felt in this trial but that they weren't going to share with a room full of strangers. This was a futile exercise in tradition, and Brigham wished they just did a random lottery instead.

When the attorneys were allowed to ask questions of the pool, Debra spent nearly forty-five minutes going through detailed personal aspects of each juror—what political party they affiliated with, what sports teams they liked, what magazines they read.

There were generalizations that had become fact in the

minds of lawyers: liberals tended to acquit, women were more likely to convict than men. Brigham hadn't seen either to be true, but Debra was playing into the stereotypes she'd been trained in.

When it was Brigham's turn, he simply stood in front of the jury pool and asked, "If I presented evidence to you that Ted Montgomery did not commit this crime, would you acquit him?"

He knew the people who would convict no matter what wouldn't be honest. That wasn't why he asked. He just wanted to get the thought into the jurors' minds that there was evidence that Ted was innocent.

After that question, he sat back down.

More formalities followed, and when they were done, the judge called for a ten-minute break before the State's first witness.

They rose as the judge, eight jurors, and two alternates left the courtroom. When they were gone, Ted looked at Brigham and said, "I'm going to take a quick walk with my kids."

Brigham nodded and sat back down, staring at the bench. He glanced behind him and saw Molly in the audience. Their eyes locked, but neither of them spoke. He turned back around, his eyes forward.

"Is there anything you need me to do?" Rebecca asked.

"Take notes if something stands out."

She hesitated. "For what it's worth, that was wrong, what she did."

Brigham didn't respond.

The ten minutes passed in silence, and Ted was back in his chair as the judge came out. Everyone rose and sat back down, and the judge said, "All right, Ms. Flynn, an opening statement if you'd like to provide one."

34

Debra Flynn stood up and walked to the lectern. She turned it to face the jury, giving Brigham a view of her opening statement: bullet points. Many attorneys used the same technique of turning the lectern toward the jury and reading off a list. It was thorough and prevented them from missing something. But Brigham thought it was damaging. It created distance between them and the jury and placed a physical object in the middle.

"On November the second of last year, Ted Montgomery ended his wife's life. Ruby Montgomery was his wife of nearly twenty years. They had three children together: Monica, Devan, and David. By all accounts, they had a loving marriage… until Ruby Montgomery developed cancer. She was hospitalized for three weeks at the University of Utah. That man, Ted Montgomery, determined that three weeks was enough.

"On the date in question, he brought in a bag of morphine and connected it to Mrs. Montgomery's IV. She was dead less than half an hour later. And this murder wasn't committed in the darkness of night with nobody around. He brought his kids to watch. A five-, ten-, and seventeen-year-old had to watch their mother die because this man decided that he didn't want to put up with her pain anymore. I don't mean to make light of cancer—my aunt died of breast cancer, and I watched her fight valiantly to the end. But never, not once, did her husband consider killing her. They dealt with the pain the best way they knew how: with medication, and she lived until her body simply couldn't fight anymore. But we don't know how long Ruby Montgomery could've lived, because on November second, Ted Montgomery took that choice away from her. He robbed her of any chance of recovery, and of the final months or even years of her life that she could've spent with her children. And he robbed the children of their mother."

She cleared her throat and stepped away from the lectern, getting closer to the jury one slow step at a time. "I know some of you may be thinking, 'Well, he killed her to alleviate her pain.' Did he? Or did he kill her to alleviate his own pain? Mrs. Montgomery never signed a do-not-resuscitate order. The defendant made that decision on his own. And the evidence today will show you overwhelmingly that he killed her because she had become too much of a burden for him. This had nothing to do with Ruby Montgomery. This act was about Ted Montgomery. So I will be asking you, after you hear the overwhelming evidence, including a confession given to police, to convict Ted Montgomery of homicide."

Brigham waited until she had taken her seat. The opening was clear and concise. It laid out the facts and painted a picture.

The typical defense strategy was to take issue with every point made by the prosecution. But that wasn't his strategy. This case wasn't about facts.

He got up and went to the courtroom's DVD player. He removed a disc from a paper sleeve and inserted it into the DVD player. Without a word, he hit play and the video began on the large-screen television against the wall.

"This is Ruby Montgomery, early in her cancer diagnosis."

On the screen, Ruby lay in a hospital bed. She had a full head of beautiful brown hair, and she was smiling as she played with Devan. David was running around in the background, and every once in a while Monica would ask a question of her mother from behind the camera phone. Ted didn't appear in the video.

Ruby seemed young and full of life, with strength and resolve—a resolve that she would survive. It came through as clearly as anything else in the video. Brigham let the jury watch it for about thirty seconds before he paused it and said, "And this is Ruby Montgomery near the end of her life." He switched to the next scene.

The image changed, and the timbre of a scream filled the courtroom. The scream was so harsh that one of the jurors gasped.

Ruby was strapped down in a bed. Her once-long hair was falling out in clumps. She was yelling and crying as a nurse injected something into her IV. Ruby screamed again, so loud that her voice nearly went hoarse.

Ted was in this video. He was sitting next to his wife, holding her hand and telling her it was almost over, that she just needed to hang on a little longer.

Ruby arched her back and screamed again, and Ted snapped at the nurse. "Damn it, give her something!"

"Sir, I'm trying."

Ted turned to his wife. "Shh, be calm, calm."

"Ted," she screamed, "please. Please."

There was no request that came with the plea. She just kept repeating, "Please, please." Brigham let it play to the end of the video and then turned it off. He approached the jury slowly, letting the video sink in. He put his hands in his pockets, making sure they could see his watch.

"That video was taken by Ruby and Ted's daughter, Monica. She, along with her father and two brothers, watched Ruby Montgomery go from the beautiful, vivacious woman you saw to a woman who howled in pain, day and night, a woman the doctors said had no chance of surviving this ordeal. See, what the government didn't tell you was that Ruby didn't just have cancer, she had one of the most painful, deadly forms of cancer that ever cursed us: pancreatic cancer. The pain was so intense, Ted will tell you, that there were times when she would just pass out from it. And when she woke, she would just start screaming again. Ted isn't a murderer. He loved his wife. He wanted to grow old with her, to sit on some porch swing and have their grandchildren running around them. But that's not what life had for them. Instead, life had the most pain a single person could go through. Both for her, and for him.

"Ted Montgomery… loved his wife. The pain was so much that she begged him to end her life. Imagine that. Imagine a pain so brutal that you no longer feel life is worth living. And then imagine being the husband of someone in that much pain. What would you do?"

Brigham had planned on discussing diminished capacity in the opening but decided against it. He would be going for the straight acquittal based on Timothy's testimony.

"I'm not asking you to judge, I'm asking you to understand. Understand what these poor people went through. I'm asking you to walk in their shoes, and to truly feel what it would be like to be put in Ted Montgomery's situation. What… would *you* do?"

He sat back down.

The judge said, "Ms. Flynn, your first witness."

Brigham waited as Debra Flynn checked something on her tablet. She could make a single important choice when it came to witness order: where to put the detective. The detective was the authority and summary of her case, a professional witness who knew how to get the facts they needed across to the jury. She could put him up first to provide an outline, to frame the case, or she could put him up last to tie up loose ends and bring the entire case together.

"Your Honor, the State calls Detective Henry Sean to the stand."

The detective approached the stand and was sworn in. He had been seated next to the prosecution as the case manager. The prosecutors could pick one of the police officers involved in any case and have the officer sit at the prosecution table and hear all the testimony, when witnesses were otherwise excluded from the courtroom.

It was the defense who typically made the motion to exclude. Brigham didn't want any witnesses excluded. He wanted everyone to hear what he was about to say.

He reached into his satchel and removed his notes. On top was another disc labeled "Detective Sean bribe." He held the disc in his hand, feeling its smooth edges. He would destroy the detective's career by playing this for the court. The media were here, so it would be on every station as the top story. His only concern was that he hadn't provided it to the prosecution because he wanted to surprise them with it. That meant his top two pieces of evidence, Tim and this disc, had been kept from the State. The rules of evidence were clear: no notice was required for impeaching someone who was lying. But the judge wasn't stupid. She would know Brigham had purposely withheld the disc and Timothy.

The judge could then declare a mistrial. Not a completely bad option, as Brigham wanted a continuance anyway to prepare fully. The risk was that Timothy seemed on edge and uncertain, and the word "prison," something Brigham shouldn't have said, had frightened him. It was completely within the realm of possibility that he would flee to Oregon and not come back if this case was set out three months. Brigham had him here now, and he would have to use that.

What the judge could also do was even more damaging: she could exclude Timothy's testimony. It would eventually be overturned on appeal, if for nothing else than an ineffective-assistance-of-counsel claim that Brigham should've given notice, but in the meantime, Ted might be sitting in jail.

If he introduced just one or the other, the disc or Tim's testimony, the judge might buy the argument that he was just ready with impeachment evidence that the prosecution should've figured out on her own. But if he tried to introduce two pieces of powerful evidence that way, Judge Lawrence might see it as a pattern that he was trying to hide the ball from the prosecution.

"Please state and spell your name for the record, Detective," Debra asked.

"Henry Nicolas Sean, that's H E…"

Brigham zoned out, his eyes on the disc. The detective really wasn't going to say anything too damaging other than discussing the confession. But the confession was part of Brigham's case that Ted was covering for his brother. It wasn't worth risking Timothy's testimony being excluded and looking deceptive to the judge just to introduce a disc with this detective accepting a bribe and doing coke. But he also couldn't let this guy be on the streets anymore. Who knew what he was accepting that bribe for—turning away from a murder? Not arresting the perpetrator when he knew who it was? Someone like that couldn't hold a gun and a badge. Brigham would gladly defend him on any charges that came about, but he couldn't just let him loose on the public.

Detective Sean went through his resumé, how many years he'd been with the police, how many homicides he'd investigated. Everything gave the jury the impression that he was professional and objective and not just a witness for the prosecution, which he actually was.

"Tell us what you remember about November second of last year," Debra said.

The detective took a drink of water out of a paper cup. "I was at my desk in the morning finishing up some paperwork when I got a call from another detective, Detective Jim Graves, that there had been a homicide at the University of Utah

Hospital. I was called out and I met Detective Graves at the entrance. He informed me that a man had told him that he had—"

"Objection, hearsay," Brigham said.

"Sustained," the judge said.

The detective glanced at the prosecution, and Debra nodded for him to go on.

"Um, well, I met Detective Graves and he told me what was going on. I entered the hospital and was led up to a room in the Huntsman Cancer Institute, which is in a different building. There's a bridge connecting the two. I found two uniformed officers sitting with the defendant, Ted Montgomery."

"And by defendant who do you mean?"

"The man at the defense table in the suit with the blue tie."

"And that is the man you saw in the hospital that day?"

"It is."

"Your Honor, I would like it noted that the detective has identified Mr. Ted Montgomery, the defendant."

"Any objection?"

Brigham rose. "No objection as to identity."

"So noted."

Debra continued. "So what happened then?"

"I approached Mr. Montgomery and stood in front of him. I asked him if he knew why I was there that day, and he said,

'Because I just killed my wife.'"

"Were those his exact words?"

"Let me check my report…" The detective picked up the sheets of paper in front of him and flipped through them. "Yes, those were his exact words. 'I just killed my wife.'"

"So then what did you do?"

The detective glanced at the jury and then kept his eyes on the prosecutor again. "I asked him what had happened. He informed me that his wife had been dying of cancer, that she'd been in an extraordinary amount of pain the past three weeks, and that she had asked him to end her suffering."

"What did you take 'end her suffering' to mean?"

"He basically told me that his wife had asked him to end her life and he had done so."

"How did he say he did it?"

"He informed me that he had brought in a bag, a medical IV bag, and hooked it up to the victim's IV. She was injected with the morphine which ended her life. The doctor informed me that the amount of morphine—"

"Objection," Brigham bellowed, "hearsay."

"Sustained," the judge said again, without looking at the detective.

Debra said, "Let's just focus on what you saw and heard, not what other people told you. The doctor is here and will be testifying, so I'd just like to know more about your impressions,

Detective."

"Of course. I'm just trying to give the jury context."

"So tell us what happened after he told you what he did."

"He said several times that he had done it, um, he repeated that his wife was in so much pain that he just couldn't stand it anymore and that they'd decided together that this was the best option. I have made a recording of the incident."

"Let's play that now." She looked to Brigham for an objection because she hadn't laid enough foundation for the recording, but he didn't object. There was no point going through recognizing the voices and the time, date, and location.

A digital recorder was hooked up to the sound system and began playing. Brigham had heard the recording. Half of it was irrelevant, and the other half was what the detective had just testified to.

Ted's voice came over the sound system as he described what had happened. He said he'd hooked up the morphine and had to play with it because he didn't know how to get it to go. That the drip was slow but eventually his wife had a smile and they spent their last few minutes together as a family laughing and reminiscing right before she died.

Debra stopped the audio and said, "Where this recording left off, what happened then?"

"The medical examiner was there as well as the doctors, and it was determined that Mrs. Ruby Montgomery had passed away. I then took Mr. Montgomery into custody. I placed him in handcuffs and escorted him off the premises. The children were there, all three of the couple's children, and I was going to call DCFS, but I allowed the oldest, Monica, to take the younger ones home."

"Why did you do that?"

The detective hesitated. "They'd been through enough. I didn't want them in foster care, too."

Brigham looked up, catching the detective's eyes. They held each other's gaze, and then both looked away.

"What happened then, Detective?"

"I was about to escort Mr. Montgomery to the Salt Lake Metro Jail when I decided I better call the screening prosecutor first, just to cover my bases. I called the DA's office, your office, and asked for the screening team. I spoke to Anita Madrid and explained the situation. She stated that they wouldn't be able to file charges quickly enough."

"Please explain to the jury what you mean."

He looked to the jury. "The district attorney's office has to file charges officially against a defendant within seventy-two hours of them being booked into jail. A lot of the time, because of the caseload and other factors, they can't do it in time. So the defendant is released until charges can be filed."

"So what else did Ms. Madrid tell you?"

"She informed me that this was a complex case and that

euthanasia was a—I think she called it a hot-button issue or something like that. It would take her screening team at least a few weeks to fully investigate and decide whether charges should be brought. I told her that it was clear he injected her with the morphine, but she said she wanted to speak with her boss before deciding anything. It was then that the decision was made that we would not take Ted Montgomery into custody until the DA's office was ready to file."

"So you let him go?"

"Yes, that's correct. We allowed him to go home with his children. Well, we were going to. When I went to speak to him and let him know, he was already gone. I didn't go after him because of my conversation with the screening team."

"So he ran?"

"Objection," Brigham said.

"Overruled."

"So he ran?" Debra asked again.

"Yes, he wasn't there when I went back to tell him we were letting him go." He cleared his throat. "When charges were eventually filed and a warrant issued, he had fled the home and was in hiding for about four days before turning himself in."

"Detective, in your testimony and on the recording, Ted stated that his wife had asked him to end her life. Did you find any witnesses to corroborate this?"

"No, we couldn't find any other witnesses that had actually heard her say that. To be fair, he had informed me before I started recording that he was the only one in the room with her during those conversations. There is a video taken by one of his children where she seems to be pleading with him which I'm sure you'll play for the jury, but it's unclear what she's asking for. Other than that, no, there is no evidence that Mrs. Montgomery had asked that he end her life."

"Did he ever say that he was remorseful about what happened?"

"No, he did not. He seemed shaken up by it, but he didn't express remorse, no."

"Thank you, Detective. No further questions."

35

Brigham held the detective's gaze as he rose and went to the lectern. He held the disc in his hand, and his eyes drifted down to it before he asked, "You ever been disciplined for misconduct, Detective Sean?"

"No."

"Not once?"

"Not ever, no."

"You ever taken bribes?"

"Objection," Debra said, shooting to her feet. "Relevance."

Brigham said, "I'm getting to that, Your Honor."

"Get to it quickly then, Mr. Theodore," she said.

Brigham looked to the detective again. "Please answer the question. Ever taken any bribes?"

"Of course not."

"Ever done cocaine while on duty?"

The detective froze. His eyes were fixed on Brigham for what seemed like a long time while he didn't speak. "No," he finally said, quieter this time.

"I'm sorry, was that a no?"

"No, I have never done cocaine."

Brigham ran his hand along the edge of the disc. This was tricky either way. Whatever he chose could blow up in his face. But he thought that the primary thing to get in was Timothy's testimony. If it bought credibility with the judge by not sandbagging the prosecutor with this disc, he had to risk it. He placed the disc on the defense table.

"Just curious," he said. "Clerk, could you please start the recording again that Ms. Flynn just played? Right toward the end."

Ted's voice came back over the sound system a moment later. He mumbled a few things and then wept. He wept a long time, and then the recording ended.

"Was that Mr. Montgomery's voice, Detective?"

"Yes, it was."

"He was crying, wasn't he?"

"Yes."

"A portion of his interview that the government didn't want the jury to hear, isn't that right?"

"Objection!" Debra shouted as she rose.

"Withdrawn," Brigham said, not wanting to argue a point he knew he would lose. "How'd Ted seem to you?"

"Seem to me?"

"Yeah, you said he appeared shaken up. How so?"

"He was trembling, his hands were trembling, and he had this stare like he was looking past us."

"Would you say he looked like he was in shock?"

The detective nodded. "Yes, that would describe it accurately."

"You stated you've done hundreds of homicide investigations. People who take another person's life, do they appear in shock and then cry afterward?"

"Well, sometimes."

"What times would those be? When they feel remorse?"

"Yes, I suppose so."

"So it's fair to say Ted felt bad about what he'd done?"

"Yes."

"It was a painful thing for him to do."

"Yes, I would imagine so."

"You think it's fair to say he didn't want to do it?"

"No, I wouldn't say that's fair. If he didn't want to do it, he wouldn't have."

"Really? Your wife ever screamed in pain for you to kill her, Detective?"

"Objection, relevance."

Brigham turned to the judge. "He's making assumptions about my client's state of mind. It's relevant if he's ever been through this situation."

"I'll allow it," the judge said.

"Detective, your wife ever diagnosed with cancer?"

"No."

"She ever scream in pain for you to end her life?"

"No."

"So you can't rightly say he just wouldn't have done it if he didn't want to, can you? Because you've never been in his shoes."

The detective thought a moment. "No, I guess I can't."

Brigham had about an hour of planned cross left, discussing clues to Ted's mental state and diminished capacity. As that wasn't the defense anymore, he skipped them to the very last few questions.

"Detective, you stated his children were there, correct?"

"Yes."

"And we heard him say on the recording that he'd brought his children in to be with their mother, right?"

"Yes, he did say that."

"That sound like the actions of a murderer to you? Bring in the kids to watch?"

"You'd be surprised at the actions of murderers. If they had any sense, they wouldn't kill anybody."

"You ever kill anybody?"

"Objection," Debra said, on her feet again. "I don't see the relevance of this line of questioning. The detective is not on trial."

"He just testified as to what people who kill other people are like. I'd like to know if he has experience in that."

"Sustained," the judge said.

Brigham moved on. "Did you talk to the kids?"

"Yes, they were interviewed before they left. The two younger ones were interviewed by a child-crimes detective and I interviewed Monica."

"Did they say anything about my client enjoying what he did?"

"No, I don't believe so. Monica said she wasn't there for the injection. She came after."

"So no one actually saw Ted Montgomery hook up his wife's IV with morphine, did they?"

"No, but as has been stated, he told us several times that it was him."

"Thank you, Detective, that's all I had."

The judge said, "Anything further, Ms. Flynn?"

"Detective, you stated the defendant fled into hiding when he found out a warrant had been issued for his arrest."

"Yes, that's right."

"Do innocent people run and hide in your exper—"

"Objection," Brigham bellowed, with more anger than he expected.

"Goes to consciousness of guilt, Your Honor."

"I'll allow it."

Debra continued, "In your experience, do innocent people run and hide?"

243

"No. Someone innocent usually comes forward and tries to prove to us they're innocent."

"Thank you, Detective. That's all I had."

The judge looked to Brigham. "Re-cross, Mr. Theodore?"

"No, Your Honor."

"Okay, do the parties agree that this witness may be excused?"

"Your Honor," Debra said, "we'd like to keep the detective in case of impeachment purposes against the defendant."

"Okay, Detective, please make sure that you are near the court at all times. If you wish to retake your place as case manager you may do so, but if not, just be within half an hour of the courtroom."

The judge turned to Debra and said, "Next witness, Ms. Flynn."

Detective Sean sat down next to her as Debra rose and said, "State calls Dr. Sydnie Ryan to the stand."

A tall, gaunt man in a suit made his way to the witness stand, and the clerk swore him in. He took his place, his back perfectly straight and a stone-cold expression on his face.

"Please state and spell your name for the record, Doctor."

"Dr. Sydnie Nathan Ryan. S Y…"

It wasn't lost on Brigham that he had included the title "Doctor" when asked to state his name—something he'd seen

244

from medical experts in every specialty.

"And where do you work, sir?"

"The University of Utah Huntsman Cancer Institute. I'm an oncologist."

"And were you working on November second of last year?"

"I was."

"Did you cross paths with the defendant that day?"

"I did."

"Please explain."

The doctor cleared his throat. "I had been Mrs. Montgomery's treating physician. She'd been under my care for a number of months, even before she was hospitalized. I knew the defendant through my interactions with her. He would come to her treatments and consultations, things like that."

"What was Mrs. Montgomery diagnosed with?"

"Stage three pancreatic cancer. It had moved into stage four by the time I saw her."

"And what does that mean, stage four?"

"Modern medicine breaks cancer diagnosis down into five stages, numbered zero through four. Stage zero is what we call 'in situ' cancer, where a cell develops into a localized tumor. This is usually non–life threatening, as the cancer doesn't spread. Then we have stage one, where the cancer cells have the ability to invade surrounding tissue. Stages two and three are a regional spread, where the cancer is distributed throughout the body and possibly caught in a lymph node, and possibly develops into more tumors. But the cancer cells are still localized to a great degree.

"What you asked about, stage four, is where the cancer cells have entered the bloodstream. At this point, they are spread throughout the body. We do have chemotherapy, radiation, and surgery available, but pancreatic cancer is something else entirely."

"How so, Doctor?"

"It's the deadliest form of cancer known and is nearly 100 percent fatal. The problem is that it's difficult to detect, so early intervention is rarely an option."

"After her diagnosis, how did Mrs. Montgomery's treatment go?"

"She responded well to the chemotherapy at first, but the cancer had spread too quickly for too long. We gave her and her husband a prognosis that she wouldn't survive another six months."

"That seems bleak. Was there no hope at all?"

"There's always hope, and I have heard of pancreatic cancer patients going into remission, but it's rare. I like to be honest with my patients about that."

"When you told Mr. and Mrs. Montgomery your prognosis, what was their reaction?"

"Shock, I guess. Ruby—ah, Mrs. Montgomery—began to cry. Her husband, the defendant, simply held her. I left them alone for a bit. When I came back, they had a few more questions, and then we began discussing treatment options."

"When did you make the decision to admit her?"

"About three months after the diagnosis, she had deteriorated to such a degree that we no longer felt home care was a viable option. We asked that she be admitted to the Institute so that she could have round-the-clock care."

"How did the defendant react to that?"

"He seemed upset by it. He kept asking if it was necessary. He wanted her home with the family. I informed him that he didn't have the resources to care for her anymore."

Debra paused and scanned her notes. "Doctor, were you at any point considering ending Ruby Montgomery's life?"

"No, of course not. It doesn't happen that often, but cases of remission and even full recovery are out there. If there's even a sliver of hope, I would never recommend anything as permanent as a managed death."

"So this was done against your recommendation?"

"Expressly against my recommendation. I never would've approved something like this. The fact is that there is a possibility Mrs. Montgomery could've survived. Now we'll never know for sure."

"Thank you, Doctor. That's all I had."

Brigham rose. "You mentioned 'managed death.' That's a term doctors use when they end the life of a patient at the patient's request, isn't it?"

"Well, I wouldn't quite put it in those terms, but yes, that's the essence. The treating physician administers medication, particularly pain medication, to such a degree that the risk of death increases substantially. It's an outdated practice and banned in almost every state."

"Almost, but not quite. It's legal in Washington, Oregon, Montana, and Vermont. Correct?"

"Yes. It is legal there. But again, we're talking about managed death under a treating physician. We don't want to set the precedent that any member of a patient's family can make the decision to end the patient's life."

"See, now I'm confused, because there's these things called do-not-resuscitate orders. What are those, Doctor?"

"They're orders given by the patient or their family to not take measures to revive a patient who has gone into a vegetative state or coma before cardiac arrest."

"So the family can decide whether a DNR order can be signed?"

"Yes."

"So a family can make decisions about ending the life of their loved ones."

"In that context with a DNR, yes. But not just willy-nilly."

"Willy-nilly?" Brigham said, his voice raised. "Are you saying Ted, a man who sat by his wife's bed for months listening to her scream herself hoarse, decided 'willy-nilly' to end her life?"

"No, I didn't mean it that way."

"That's exactly what you meant. You and the detective are so quick to judge him. Have you sat by your wife's bed while she begged for you to take her life?"

"Objection," Debra said.

Brigham stepped closer to the witness. "I bet you wouldn't be using terms like 'willy-nilly' to describe your own wife dying of what you described as 'the most painful cancer there is.'"

"Objection, Your Honor. He is badgering the witness. Not to mention—"

"Badgering a witness that sits up there and says things like 'willy-nilly' to describe the most painful decision my client's ever had to make."

The judge held up a hand. "Enough, both of you. Mr. Theodore, please stick to what's relevant, and let's stay away from conjecture and what the doctor would do in various circumstances."

Brigham paced the space between the attorney tables and the judge's bench, the anger rising in his guts. The sense of self-righteousness from the detective and doctor was too much. Neither of them could picture himself in that situation, hearing the person he loved begging to die.

"So a DNR says it's okay for a family to decide when not to revive a patient, correct?"

"Yes."

"And there's no question that the family can decide that."

"No. It only becomes the family's right if the patient is unconscious or otherwise unable to decide."

"What if the patient doesn't want to be resuscitated and the family agrees? That's gotta be just fine, right? Since both the patient and family agree?"

"Certainly."

"So under that scenario, it's just fine, but because my client didn't sign a piece of paper, it's murder? Is that what you're saying?"

"Not reviving and taking affirmative action to end someone's life are two completely separate things."

"You ever let someone die who could've been revived?"

"Objection, relevance."

Brigham said, "He just said it's different. Let's hear if he actually has done it and so knows the difference."

"Overruled."

"Thank you, Judge," Brigham said. "Now, Doctor, have you ever let someone die who you could've saved?"

"Of course I have. Every oncologist has. We follow the directions of the patient and the patient's family in those circumstances."

"Did Ruby Montgomery ever ask for you to kill her?"

"Not in a serious manner. She was overwhelmed with pain and would say things hinting about that."

"Hinting? What do you mean hinting?"

"She would say she wanted it all to be over with, but then the next day, when the pain subsided, she would want to fight. It's common in patients near death to make such proclamations."

"Did she come to you and talk to you seriously about ending her life?"

"No, I don't believe so."

"No. She went to her husband, didn't she?"

"Supposedly."

"And the husband came to you?"

"Yes, he approached me, but I turned him down."

"And that's the real issue, isn't it? Doctors can kill and let people die and it's just fine, but if family members do it, they're arrested for murder."

"Objection, Your Honor. I don't see the point of any of this."

Brigham turned to her, his face flushed hot with anger. "Of course you don't because you weren't next to her bed listening to her scream."

"Mr. Theodore," the judge said sternly, "that is enough."

Brigham held his tongue in check. He turned away from the judge and closed his eyes for a moment. He looked at Rebecca, who motioned for him to come over. He bent over the defense table and read what she had written on a notepad. He smiled and turned back to the doctor.

"Ruby Montgomery had a do-not-resuscitate order, didn't she?"

"Yes, she did."

"And Ted and she decided this together."

"Yes."

"With you?"

"Yes, I discussed it with them."

"And what did you recommend when you discussed whether to revive Mrs. Montgomery?"

The doctor hesitated. "I told them that there was little likelihood of recovery, and that she shouldn't resuscitate."

"Why?"

He hesitated again. "Because the pain is unbearable."

Brigham grinned and sat back down, glancing once at Debra. "No further questions."

Debra rose and said, "Doctor, this DNR, do you have it?"

"No, we just discussed it. Mr. Montgomery took her life before we could make it official, so to speak."

"So there was no official DNR. Would you have killed Ruby Montgomery if she had asked you to?"

"No, never. Not in a million years."

"And without a DNR you would've revived her were she to go into cardiac arrest, correct?"

"Without an official DNR, yes. I would've been obligated to revive her."

"Thank you. Nothing further."

The judge looked between the attorneys. "I think this is a good time for a break. Be back here in fifteen minutes, please."

The bailiff shouted, "All rise."

As the judge followed the jury out, Ted stepped out of the courtroom with his family. Brigham turned to Rebecca and said, "Thanks for that. It completely slipped my mind."

"No problem. You were getting so worked up, I'm not surprised you forgot something."

"I don't like how everybody's judging him without being in his place."

She glanced at the prosecution table and then to Molly, who was leaving the courtroom. "What now?"

"The nurse and then the medical examiner. That'll take the rest of the day and probably tomorrow. The State will probably rest after that and we'll put Ted up after."

"He's nice. I hope we win."

It was said so innocently, so naively, that Brigham couldn't help but grin. "So do I."

36

After the break, which Brigham used to run to the bathroom and then stare out the windows at the sunlight in the lobby for a while, he returned to find Ted in his place, speaking quietly to Rebecca. As Brigham took his place, he had to rise again as the judge walked in. She took a moment on her computer and then said, "Okay, next witness."

Debra rose from her table and said, "We call Dr. Scott Jacobs to the stand."

Scott Jacobs was an assistant medical examiner for Salt Lake County, a pathologist with twenty years' experience and known for being thorough to the point of tedium. Debra was probably saving the emotional impact of the nurse who found Ruby Montgomery dead for last.

The ME was sworn in and began by describing the chemical composition of morphine, how close it was to heroin, and its effects on the body. He then moved through a history of morphine use in euthanasia and why it was the preferred drug. This took nearly two hours, and he had barely addressed the case at hand.

The next two hours were about the actual autopsy and

then the toxicology report. Four and a half hours passed, and Brigham knew Judge Lawrence would continue the testimony into tomorrow. He hoped the ME would wrap it up soon.

After five hours and two bathroom breaks, he looked down at the notes he had. The only issue was the time of death, which Dr. Jacobs determined was between noon and one o'clock. Brigham wanted to make sure he had him down on the actual time to show that Timothy could've injected the morphine and then fled.

Finally, after having established that Ruby Montgomery was actually dead from a morphine overdose administered on November second, Debra stopped asking him questions. Brigham rose, and the judge said, "Mr. Theodore, I'm inclined to stop for the day as it's nearing six o'clock."

"Just a couple questions, Your Honor."

"Okay. If it goes any longer we'll have to start with it tomorrow."

"Understood." He took to the lectern. "You said time of death was between noon and one o'clock?"

"That's correct."

"But you can't say for certain when within that hour the injection occurred?"

"To a medical certainty? No, I can't. An hour's about as good as it can get."

"Thank you, Dr. Jacobs. Nothing further."

The judge adjourned court for the day. The jury was not going to be sequestered and would be allowed to go home. But the judge asked them not to speak about the case to anyone, even their spouses, something Brigham knew was impossible.

"All rise for the jury," the bailiff called.

Brigham rose, as did everyone else, as they were escorted out. Debra packed up her things and left without saying anything. Brigham turned to Ted and said, "I'll see you in the morning." He looked to Timothy, who nodded to him and he nodded back.

Molly hadn't returned after the break, but Brigham still searched the courtroom for her.

"You wanna grab something to eat?" Rebecca asked.

He looked at her, held her gaze a moment, and looked away. Watching Ted put his arms around his children and walk out of the courtroom, Brigham said, "I could actually use a drink."

The bar was far enough from downtown that they wouldn't see anyone they knew. Brigham walked in first and held the door open for Rebecca. She came in, crossed the space like she owned it, and sat down in a booth. He followed.

The waitress came over and brought menus. Brigham asked for a beer and Rebecca a cosmopolitan.

"You didn't play the video," she said when the waitress had left.

"Too risky. I didn't want to jeopardize Timothy's testimony."

"Might be ineffective assistance not to present that video to the jury."

He shrugged. "It's okay. We're not gonna win because the detective did coke. We're gonna win if the jury believes Tim."

"You think there's a chance they *won't* believe him?"

"Yeah. A younger brother defending his role model? I could see it."

"Wow. Even with someone else taking responsibility, there's a chance our guy could go to prison. Seems like the whole system is stacked against us."

"It is. And we have fewer rights over the decades rather than more. In thirty years, I think the criminal justice system will be unrecognizable. There are people in Congress and the judiciary that think individuals shouldn't have any rights when it comes to public safety."

"But you don't believe that."

He shook his head as the waitress set his beer down. "No. I'm scared of an unethical government, not an unethical person. There's little damage one unethical person can do compared to what a government can do when it no longer has morality as a hindrance."

They chatted over their meal. The conversation was pleasant enough if a little stilted. Brigham couldn't think about anything but the trial, and she kept talking about places she'd been to on vacation and things she'd like to do. He nodded and asked questions where appropriate, but ultimately he could think of nothing but Ted Montgomery behind bars.

When they were finished, Brigham told her he would see her tomorrow. She looked as though she wanted to ask him something, but he didn't give her the chance. He got onto his bike, which he insisted on riding rather than letting her drive him, and rode back into Salt Lake City as darkness fell.

Back in town, he got the text message from Jen he'd been waiting for since after the trial let out and he'd contacted her. He replied "thank you" and rode up to Rose Park to the address she'd given.

The home was dilapidated. It had been painted white once, but now the paint was chipping so profusely that he could hardly tell. The screen door creaked as he opened it and knocked.

Detective Henry Sean answered in shorts with a beer in his hand. The two men glared at each other but said nothing until Sean said, "You may as well come in, I guess."

Brigham followed him inside. The home wasn't necessarily dirty but was so cluttered that it appeared so. On the coffee table were three empty beer bottles. Brigham took a seat on the couch as Sean sat in the recliner. He'd been watching a basketball game and turned it down with the remote.

"How'd you find out?" Sean asked.

"Someone recorded it."

"What's on it?"

"You snorting coke and accepting a bag from some guy who looks like he just got out of prison. There was some talk of getting hookers later, too."

He nodded and took a sip of his beer. "How much do you want?"

"How much what?"

He looked at him. "Money, Counselor. How much do you want?"

"I don't want money."

"Well, you want something, otherwise you would've turned it over to Internal Affairs or used it in court."

"I thought about it."

"Why didn't you?"

"Because you let the kids go home."

Sean finished his beer and set the bottle down on the coffee table. "If you don't want money, what do you want?"

"You can't be a cop anymore."

"What the hell are you talking about?"

"I'm not going to turn this in. But you're going to quit the force. Tomorrow. I don't care what reason you give them. But

259

you can't be a cop anymore."

He shook his head. "I make fifty-two thousand a year. Biting away at that is two alimony payments, two child support payments, and a mortgage. By the end of the month, I got exactly $168 left for clothes, food, gas, and dates. I was just sick of eating Top Ramen every night."

"How'd it start?"

"Little things here and there. Few hundred bucks if I didn't execute a warrant on someone, things like that."

"How'd it go to bags of cash?"

He swallowed. "You just get used to the money, you know? And then the thought of going back and having nothing is just unbearable, and you'll do anything not to go back to that."

Brigham leaned forward. "I feel for you, but you can't be a cop anymore."

"You little shit. What the hell do you—"

"I've starved, too. I didn't take a dime from anyone to help me, much less money from thugs. You swore to protect these people, and you're their worst enemy now."

Sean looked away, to the television. He was quiet for a second before saying, "Give me a year to find another job."

"No, you'll quit tomorrow. Or this disc goes straight to IAD." Brigham rose. "I'm sorry, but that's the most courtesy I can show you."

Brigham left the house, hoping he wasn't about to catch a bullet in the back. As he shut the door, he caught a glimpse of Sean staring blankly at the television, his head hung low, his arm reaching for another beer.

37

The next morning, Sean wasn't at court. Debra looked around several times, and Brigham knew she was looking for him. Finally, after delaying as long as she could, when everyone was settled back in court, Debra stood and said, "We'd like to call Gabriella Mecham to the stand."

Brigham watched as a woman in scrubs marched to the witness stand as if she were carrying out a general's orders in the military. She was sworn in and took her seat. After the preliminary questions, she recounted how she had walked into the room when Ruby Montgomery had flatlined.

"I didn't think anything of it, at first. Patients pull off their monitors all the time, or they slip off... I just thought that's what happened. But when I came in, I saw Ted Montgomery standing over the bed staring down at his wife with their three kids surrounding him. The kids were crying. It was when I saw Ruby that I knew. She was still. Just completely still. Like a statue. And I knew she was gone and that he had killed her."

"What did he say to you?" Debra asked.

"He told me he just wanted her to have peace. But ain't no

one gonna find peace bein' murdered by her husband."

"Objection," Brigham said.

"Sustained."

Debra said, "Nurse Mecham, what happened next?"

"He just kept sayin' 'she looked so peaceful.' I checked her and there was no pulse. I hit the emergency button and set off the alarm. Everybody ran in. We gave her shots of adrenaline and everything, but nothin' worked. She'd been dead too long. There was no official DNR in place, so we tried to revive her the best we could. Maybe twenty minutes. She was already brain dead, though, by the time we got there."

"So what did you do after trying to revive her?"

"I called the police. I don't tolerate murderers in my hospital."

"Objection," Brigham said, standing this time.

"Sustained."

Debra read something on her tablet. "What happened after the police were called?"

"They interviewed him and he confessed to doing it. But it was the children I felt bad for, that they had this murdering son of a bitch as a father."

"Your Honor!" Brigham shouted, getting to his feet.

"Nurse Mecham," the judge said, "please keep your opinions to yourself and tell us what happened."

Debra chimed in, "Did he seem remorseful to you?"

263

"No, not one bit. It was like he was out for a walk in the park. Like he didn't care at all. And I had never heard her once say she wanted to die. She wanted to fight. She was a fighter. She just didn't know she was married to a murderer."

"Your Honor, this is ridiculous."

"Keep your pants on, Mr. Theodore." She turned to Debra. "Ms. Flynn, does the witness have anything other than insults to add?"

"I think I can be done now, Your Honor."

"Okay, your witness, Mr. Theodore."

Brigham rose and approached her. He stood three feet away, close enough that he could smell her perfume. "You said Ruby Montgomery never asked to die, is that right?"

"That's right. Never heard it once."

"How many patients do you have in your section of the hospital on a typical night?"

"I don't know, it varies."

"Guess."

"Maybe twenty. Twenty-five."

"Twenty-five patients. So how many hours a day do you get to spend with each of these twenty-five patients on an eight-hour shift?"

"It's not the time—"

"How many?" Brigham said sternly, stepping a foot closer to her.

"Maybe fifteen minutes each. Maybe more."

"Fifteen minutes? You saw Ruby Montgomery for fifteen minutes every night and you have the audacity to say she *never* said she wanted to end her life?"

"I ain't never heard it once from her."

"How many patients have died under your care?"

"What? What does that have to do with anything?"

"How many patients have died while you were their nurse, Ms. Mecham?"

"I don't know."

"Take another guess."

She looked to the prosecutor but received no help. "I don't know. Maybe a hundred or so over the years. Working in oncology is like that."

"And of those hundred, did you try and resuscitate each one?"

"No, of course not."

"Of course not. Because they had DNR orders. Orders not to save them."

"I don't understand your point. It's two different things."

"They wanted to die and you let them die. You stood by when you could've saved them, and you let them die. This man," he said, pointing to Ted, "doesn't want his wife screaming every second she's awake, so he lets her die peacefully with her family instead of withering away to nothing, and you're telling me it's not the same thing?"

"He murdered her," she said loudly. "He ripped her away from this life like some executioner. She could've had a lot more time. She could've survived."

He came over and placed his hands on the witness box, staring the nurse in the eyes. "She had a DNR, even if it wasn't official and wasn't notarized and signed. If she had it signed, and slipped into a coma, you would've stood by and watched her die, wouldn't you? Just like you watched a hundred other people die. Who's the executioner?"

"Objection!"

"Sustained. Counselor—"

"I know, Judge. Withdrawn."

Brigham sat down. Nurse Mecham was fidgeting on the stand, her cheeks the color of a red crayon. Debra stood up and asked, "Was there a possibility, in your experience, that Ruby Montgomery could've survived if Ted Montgomery hadn't killed her?"

"Yes, without a doubt in my mind."

"Thank you. Nothing further, Your Honor."

"Mr. Theodore?"

"Nothing, Your Honor."

"Nurse Mecham, you are excused with our thanks." Judge Lawrence turned to Debra. "Next witness."

"The State rests, Your Honor."

"Okay, Mr. Theodore, at this point I'll turn the time over to you."

"Thank you, Your Honor. The defense would call Ted Montgomery to the stand."

"Mr. Montgomery, please come forward."

Ted rose and hesitantly shuffled over to the stand. He was sworn in and sat down, unable to look anyone in the eyes. He kept his head low.

"Your name, please," Brigham said.

Ted stated and spelled his name.

"Tell us how you met your wife, Ted."

He grinned, looked up shyly for a moment and then back down. "She was the love of my life. We met in college. I was a TA for calculus, and she needed help in her math class. I was just randomly assigned to her by the college. Total fate. I think we were married a year later. Really fast. Few years after that we had our first child, my daughter, Monica. Best day of my life."

"How long were you guys married?"

"Over twenty years. She got sick on our twentieth anniversary."

"What do you mean?"

"That was the first night she complained about a pain in her abdomen, in her side. She said it was radiating and she thought she might have a kidney stone or something. We ignored it for a while, maybe like two weeks. She took ibuprofen and put up with the pain." He paused. "She didn't like hospitals. It was always a chore to get her to go to them. But I finally talked her into it. They did some tests and said they were worried. We came back the next day and they did a… CT scan, needle biopsy. That's what they said it was. She stayed in the CT scanner, and the doctor shoved a needle into her abdomen for a tissue sample." He stopped and looked down a long time before saying, "Three days later, they told us she had tumors the size of a quarter."

"What did you guys do?"

"Um, we discussed the different treatment options. The cancer was really advanced at this point. It had spread all over her body. She began the chemo and the pills, the radiation treatments… it seemed to ease things for maybe two weeks. After that, things just got worse and worse."

"How?"

"The pain, for one. The pain medications she was on stopped being effective. She got to doses so high the doctors were nervous she might overdose, so they cut her back. Marijuana might've worked, but it's not legal in this state. So we didn't really have anything. I mean, by the time she was admitted to the hospital, she was either screaming or crying. She couldn't eat, couldn't do anything. I took a leave of absence from work to be with her and…" He choked up, and in an instant the tears began to flow. "I never saw anyone in so much pain." He breathed deeply, as though he couldn't draw breath. "And I couldn't do anything. I just held her hand and begged them for more medicine. What else could I do?"

"How long did this last?"

"Three weeks, maybe more. The doctors told us she was likely to be dead in ninety days, and definitely wouldn't survive past six months. At that point we were really just waiting for the end. One day, she just turned to me and she was crying from the pain, and she just… she just asked if I could help her end it. She said she knew I would do it for her. We discussed it a few more times after that. And the pain was just getting worse and worse… she was so tired. She just wanted peace. That's all. Just peace. And I gave that to her. No matter what happens to me, she has peace."

"Where'd you get the morphine?"

Ted looked at him. He was silent a moment. "I don't remember."

"You don't remember where you got the morphine that supposedly killed your wife?"

"No, some guy. I don't know who."

Brigham stepped into the well and paced around a little. "Do you have a criminal record?"

"No, you know I don't."

"Ever been in trouble before for anything?"

He shook his head. "No."

"And just outta the blue, you knew a guy who could get you enough morphine to kill somebody?"

"Yes."

Brigham nodded. "No further questions."

Debra looked at him as if he were crazy. She stood up and took the lectern. "Did you give your wife an overdose of morphine, Mr. Montgomery?"

"Yes."

"Did the doctors tell you to do it?"

"No."

"You did it on your own?"

"Yes, in consultation with my wife."

"Did anyone hear your wife ask for that other than you?"

"No. I don't think so."

"But you took her life anyway? Without making sure that somebody else knew she had asked for it?"

"I didn't think about it. I just wanted to give her peace. That's all. That's all I wanted."

"You had to leave work to take care of her?"

"Yes."

"You had to be with her all the time, didn't you? Feed her, clothe her, give her medication?"

"Yes."

"Must be quite a burden to have someone else's life in your hands like that."

"I didn't mind."

"Really?" Debra grabbed a sheet of paper off the prosecution table. "Isn't it true you once told a co-worker that it was getting to be too much? That you didn't know how much more you could help her?"

Ted hesitated. Brigham had seen the email and hoped Debra wouldn't bring it up.

"Yes," he said. "It was hard. I admit that. But I loved her."

"You knew it was illegal, didn't you? You knew that it was illegal to give her an overdose of morphine?"

"Yes."

"But you did it anyway?"

"Yes."

"And you killed her?"

"Yes."

"But she could've survived. The doctors told you there was a chance, didn't they?"

He shrugged. "I don't remember."

"You don't remember if the doctors told you there was a chance your wife could live, or you don't *want* to remember?" She stepped closer to him. "She could've lived, and instead you took her life. What if she would've survived, Mr. Montgomery? What if she would've lived? We'll never know will we? Because you killed her without waiting to see."

Ted began to weep. He put his palms to his eyes and

Debra stood there, watching him.

"Nothing further."

Brigham shook his head as the judge looked to him.

"Mr. Montgomery," the judge said, "you may step down."

Brigham rose and Ted gave him an icy stare. As he brushed past, he whispered, "What the hell are you doing? You promised me."

Brigham hesitated only a moment, long enough to see a single image in his mind: Ted Montgomery at the end of his life in a white prison jumpsuit. His children no longer visiting him, no hope left, the intelligence once so prominent in his eyes long since dulled.

"The defense would call Timothy Montgomery to the stand."

Debra was on her feet. "Your Honor, approach?"

"Certainly."

The two attorneys beelined for the judge's bench. Debra was speaking before they were even all the way there.

"I was not given notice for this witness, and I would object to their testimony."

"It's not a witness in my case-in-chief, Your Honor. I'm calling him as an impeachment witness."

"Who are you impeaching?"

"My client."

The judge paused. "You're accusing your client of lying in

front of the jury?"

"Yes."

"Mr. Theodore, that's unethical. You can't do that."

"Frankly, Judge, that's an issue decided by a Bar ethics committee, not this court. I am allowed to impeach any witness with credible evidence. And I only found out about this witness's testimony the day before the trial."

The judge said, "I don't like this. I'm going to allow it, because you're right, but I'm seriously considering being the one to file that Bar complaint against you."

"You have to do what you think is right, Judge."

She eyed him a moment. "Okay, let's see where this goes."

Debra said, "Your Honor, I have no idea what this witness is going to say. I would like a day to interview him and prepare."

"Then you better wing it because I'm not delaying this trial an entire day."

Brigham returned to the lectern as Debra sat down. Timothy was already on the stand. He looked nervous and pale and kept taking large sips of water.

"Who are you, sir?" Brigham said.

"No," Ted said, jumping to his feet. "Your Honor, I don't want this. I don't want him to testify."

"Mr. Montgomery," the judge nearly shouted, "take your seat, right now! I decide who can and cannot testify in this courtroom. Sit down. Now."

Ted, reluctantly, sat down. He lowered his eyes and didn't look up again.

"Um, Timothy Montgomery. I'm Ted's, the defendant's, brother."

"You've heard the testimony today. What did you think about it?"

Timothy hesitated. He looked over at Ted and then back to Brigham with fear in his eyes, such an intense fear that Brigham wasn't sure what he was about to say.

"It's a damn lie. Ted didn't put that morphine into her IV. I did."

A few murmurs went up, and one of the jurors mumbled something like "Shit." Brigham waited a moment, letting that sink in. He glanced at Debra, who was sitting with her arms folded across her chest, no expression on her face.

"Explain, please."

"Ruby was just so… I mean, I've never seen a change that quick. In a few weeks she was just a different person because of the pain. I couldn't even talk to her on the phone anymore. She was gone. And Ted and I talked about the conversation he had with her, about ending it, but he told me he couldn't do it. I mean, it was his wife of twenty years. What kinda man could do that? Even if she *was* in pain? So I came down. I got the morphine from this pharmacist that went to my gym. I looked up on the internet how much would kill a person."

"What did you do when you got here?"

"I went to the hospital, and I called Ted and told him what I was about to do. He begged me not to, started crying. He's always been like that. Really emotional. So I told him to get his butt down there because in fifteen minutes I was giving it to her, and she would only have about half an hour after that."

"Did he come down?"

"Yeah, he rushed down with all three kids. I'd already given it to her by the time he got there. She was really peaceful, you know? Just smiling and putting her arm around her kids. She was loopy and her eyes kept rolling into the back of her head, but she was there—the old Ruby, from before the cancer." He swallowed and looked down at the floor before staring at Ted. "The kids got to see her one more time and say goodbye."

Brigham looked over and Ted was in tears. He was trying to hold them back as well as he could, but they were flowing down his cheeks and leaving little circular wet marks on his tie.

"Why would you do this, Tim? Ted asked you not to."

"I know, but I knew it was for the best. And I knew he couldn't do it, even if he knew it was for the best, too. Someone had to. No person deserves to go through that much pain. No one. Someone had to help her, and her so-called doctors basically just said, 'tough, suck it up.' Someone had to help her." He looked to the jury. "I love my brother. But I'm not lying about this. He tried to protect me. He said that I was younger and I have a baby on the way. I'm up here knowing that I will probably be arrested over this. But I can't let him go down for something I did. I killed Ruby Montgomery. Ted had nothing to do with it. And you shoulda seen her face when I told her why I was there. She was so happy. Just so... damn happy that it was over."

Brigham stood a moment at the lectern just to allow the words to hang in the air. Then he said, "Nothing further," and sat down.

Debra was motionless, as though she hadn't even realized Brigham's direct had ended. Then she rose and bypassed the lectern so she could stand right in front of Timothy. "You guys are brothers?"

"Yes, ma'am."

"You don't look that much alike."

"Same father, different mothers."

She paced near the jury and then stopped. "So you drove all the way down from Oregon to kill your sister-in-law?"

"End her suffering. She was suffering more than I'd ever seen anyone suffer."

"And you just happened to know someone who could get you morphine on the fly?"

"Yes. I know people who know people. It wasn't that

hard."

"And yet there's no mention of you ever having come to visit Ruby. No sign-ins, no witnesses that saw you there."

"I was family, and no, they didn't have any place to sign in. You would get to these double doors and the secretary or whatever would buzz you in. She checked my ID and then asked Ruby if it was okay, and she said yes."

"What room was she in?"

"Um, I don't remember."

"What was she wearing?"

"Like, a hospital gown."

"What color?"

He hesitated. "I think it was blue."

"Was her hair done up or was it just hanging down?"

"I don't remember."

"Was the television on?"

"How the hell am I supposed to remember that?"

Debra stepped closer to him. "You're saying you killed this woman and you don't even remember what she was wearing? That seems like the kind of thing you'd remember. Unless of course you make a habit of going around killing people in hospitals."

"Objection," Brigham said.

"Sustained."

Debra paced a bit more. "Which wrist was the hospital ID

277

tag wrapped around?"

He shrugged. "I don't know. Left, I think."

"How many chairs were in the room?"

"Two."

She placed her hands on the witness box, staring at him. "Which arm was her IV in?"

Timothy hesitated. "The left."

She nodded and sat back down. "No further questions."

"Redirect, Mr. Theodore," the judge said.

"None."

"Okay, well, Mr. Montgomery, you may step down. Next witness, Counselor."

"Actually, Your Honor," Debra said, "before he continues, I have an impeachment witness of my own. I would like to recall Nurse Mecham to the stand. And she stated if I needed her again it would take her about half an hour to get down here."

Brigham looked at the judge. An impeachment witness could go up at anytime, and the preferred time was right after the testimony of the witness they were impeaching. But he didn't want to stop the flow of testimony. All he had left was Monica, and he wanted to get her in right after Timothy, but he certainly didn't want Nurse Mecham to be the last witness the jury heard.

"No objection," Brigham said.

"Okay," the judge said as she looked to the jury. "Ladies and gentlemen of the jury, we are going to take, well, let's just say an hour break so you can get something to eat. We'll consider this an early lunch. Please be back here in exactly one hour and, again, do not discuss this case with anyone else."

The court rose for the jury as they filed out. Brigham looked at Ted, whose eyes were down on the table. He said in almost a whisper, "I didn't want this. He has his whole life ahead of him."

Brigham turned and walked out of the courtroom, not waiting for anyone else. His stomach was growling, but more than food, he just wanted to be alone, to find somewhere to zone out and run everything through in his mind.

A Mexican restaurant around the corner had decent food, but they'd been closed several times for health code violations. Not many people went there. Brigham had a sneaking suspicion it was just a front business for something seedier.

He didn't see a rack for his bike there, so he rolled it inside and leaned it against the wall. A hostess seated him at a table by the window. Two Hispanic men in greasy overalls with dirt caked under their nails spoke quietly in Spanish, and no music was playing.

Brigham ordered a cheese quesadilla, figuring there was no way he could get food poisoning from it, and a Sprite. He stared out the windows so long that he was actually surprised when his food came.

He ate in silence and then just sat there, watching the people on the sidewalks and the cars in the street. Salt Lake had become his home, but he still felt like a foreigner sometimes, placed there out of the blue and trying too hard to fit in. He had an irrational fear that everyone could see this, too, and knew he was a fraud.

He rose and hurried back to the courthouse with ten minutes to spare. Nurse Mecham was in the hallway with Debra and gave him an icy glare. He ignored them and entered the courtroom. Rebecca was already at the defense table, but Ted wasn't.

She looked at him and raised her eyebrows. "This is nuts. They never taught you this stuff in trial ad."

"They don't teach you much in law school. Much you can use, anyway."

The doors opened and Ted came in. He looked sullen, weak. He sat between them and didn't say anything. Brigham didn't have anything to say to him, either, and the three of them sat in silence. Rebecca said, "I read about this fungus that, like, zombifies ants. It's really interesting, actually. Apparently it takes over their brains and has them perform things they don't want to do."

Brigham looked over at her and then forward again. She cleared her throat and mumbled something under her breath, but neither man said anything.

The judge came out and asked if there was anything that needed to be addressed before they brought the jury out. Debra rose and said, "One issue, Your Honor. I have another impeachment witness, as well. Devan Montgomery."

Brigham was on his feet. "He's ten years old and has nothing relevant to add."

"Timothy Montgomery has claimed that he was the one who killed the victim. Devan was there when his father admitted that he was the one who killed her. I'd like to hear from him."

"Then she should've put him on in her case-in-chief. There's no impeachment value to his testimony."

"Then I would ask for an *in-camera* review by Your Honor to determine if that's true."

The judge thought a moment. She shook her head. "I don't know. It seems like you're stretching, Ms. Flynn. But I'm happy to do an *in-camera* review."

The judge rose, and the bailiff came out and led Devan from the audience back behind the judge's bench where Debra, Brigham, and Rebecca followed. A door led to a hallway and several of the judges' offices. Judge Lawrence's was second on the right. The office was decorated with sports memorabilia from the U.S. women's soccer team.

The attorneys sat in the back of the room while Devan sat

in a chair before the judge's massive desk. The judge removed her robe, revealing a blue suit underneath, and sat down. She smiled widely at Devan and said, "Devan, how are you?"

"I'm okay," he said quietly.

"I've brought you back here because Ms. Flynn seems to think you may have some information that would be helpful for us to decide what happened to your mother. Is it all right if I ask you a few questions?"

He glanced around and then his eyes drifted down again, and he nodded.

"Okay. You were with your mother when she passed, right?"

"Yes."

"Did your father drive you there?"

He nodded.

"Did you see your uncle there?"

"No. I mean, yes. I don't know."

She nodded. "I bet this is really painful for you, isn't it?"

He nodded. "I don't want to talk up there."

"You don't want to testify?"

"No."

"Why not?"

"Because it would hurt my dad."

The judge hesitated and glanced at the lawyers. "How would it hurt your dad?"

His shoulders slumped, and Brigham heard him sob. "Because I miss my mom. She didn't have to die. That doctor said she could have lived." He wiped tears away on the back of his arm. "But I didn't see my dad do anything."

The judge's face softened. "I understand." She looked up at the attorneys. "Let's go."

Once back in the courtroom, the judge took the bench and said into the microphone, clearly for the record in case there was an appeal, "I am denying the State's motion to have Devan Montgomery testify as an impeachment witness. I do not believe he has any testimony of impeachment value, and that testifying would be more harmful to him than it would be probative to the case at hand. The defendant stated on the stand he injected the victim with morphine, and Devan would only be testifying to an act which he did not witness." She looked at the bailiff. "Please bring the jury back."

The jury was brought out, and Nurse Mecham took the stand again.

38

Gabriella Mecham was in scrubs again. She took the stand and played with her wedding ring as Debra reviewed something on her tablet.

"Nurse Mecham, you were the primary care nurse for Ruby Montgomery, is that correct?"

"For my shift, yes. We had other nurses on other shifts."

"Did you see her on the date of her death?"

"Yes, I did."

"What was her hair like?"

"Her hair?"

"Yes, her hair."

Mecham looked at the judge and then back to Debra. "Well, um, she'd lost a lot of it through radiation. So she liked to wear a bandana that covered her head."

"All of it?"

"Yes."

"What color hospital gown was she wearing on the date of her death?"

"Pink."

Debra stepped around the lectern, so close to the jury that

she placed one hand on the jury box. "This is very important that you answer this correctly, Nurse Mecham: What arm was her IV hooked into?"

"Her right."

"You're positive?"

"Yes. We couldn't get a vein in her left. I was the one who did it."

"Thank you, nothing further."

Brigham stood up. "If someone had just killed his sister-in-law, you would expect them to be shaken up and not remember everything exactly, wouldn't you?"

"Objection!"

"Withdrawn. Nothing further."

"Okay, Nurse Mecham, you may step down." The judge looked at Brigham. "Any other witnesses, Mr. Theodore?"

"Defense calls Monica Montgomery." He looked back at Monica. She had the saddest look in her eyes that he'd ever seen, somewhere between being completely lost and being completely terrified. He didn't want to put her through this, but he had to let the jury see what Ted was losing if convicted.

After being sworn in, she took her seat. She kept her eyes low, unable to look at anyone. Brigham waited a few moments, hoping she'd get more comfortable. Then he smiled at her and said, "You're Ted and Ruby's oldest daughter?"

"Yes."

"Did you actually see your father administer the morphine to your mother?"

"No."

"Did anyone see it?"

"No, I don't think so."

Brigham went to the laptop and turned on the video of Ruby screaming to Ted. He paused it and said, "Do you recognize this video?"

"Yes."

"What is it?"

"It's a video I took of my mom at the hospital. My mom and dad."

Brigham played the video. Ruby's screams filled the courtroom. The jury's eyes were glued to the screen, but Debra looked passive. The video ended and Brigham wanted to play it again, but felt he'd gotten the impact he wanted.

Brigham thought for a moment. He had hit the main point he wanted to hit, so there was no reason to put her through more of the same. "I'm sorry," was all he said before sitting down.

Debra stood up. She would have to be careful. The jury must've instantly sympathized with Monica, a girl who had lost one parent and might lose another. If Debra came at her too hard or too long, she would alienate the jury.

"Did your father tell you he was the one who hooked up

the morphine bag to your mother's IV?"

She hesitated. "Yes."

"Did you see your uncle that day at all?"

"No."

"He wasn't in the room, or out in the hall?"

"No."

"Did your father ever tell you your uncle was the one responsible for this?"

"No."

Debra nodded to the judge and sat back down.

The judge turned to the jury. When the attorneys had rested, it was time for her to go through the jury instructions. There were fifty-eight of them. The judge read each one out loud into the record. The attorneys had agreed on them days ago, and nothing in them was a surprise. Brigham kept his eyes low, his hands folded on the table. He couldn't look at Ted or anyone else.

An hour and a half passed as the judge instructed the jury on deliberations, what was and was not permissible, and how to ask for breaks or ask questions of the Court or attorneys. When she was done, she said, "I was planning on taking a break, but I think I'd like to just go into closing statements and send the jury back after a bathroom break. What do you think,

Counselors?"

"That's fine, Your Honor," Debra said.

Brigham just nodded.

"Okay, ladies and gentlemen of the jury, we will now hear closing arguments in this matter. The State will go first, followed by the defense. The State does have the opportunity for rebuttal but may waive that if they so wish. As I instructed you before, closing arguments are viewpoints of the attorneys and are not evidence. We'll begin with Ms. Flynn whenever she's ready."

Debra rose. She stood in front of the jury, her hands behind her back, confident and stern, a predator about to spring.

"This is a case about a man killing his wife to make it easy. Not to make it easy for her, but to make it easy for him. He was the one sick of dealing with her. He was the one who didn't want to give her a chance to live. He was the one who killed her.

"I know you may be thinking about the brother testifying. Don't buy it. It is a ploy by a man who set this entire thing up to lead to that moment. Ted Montgomery is an engineer—a robotics engineer who deals with complex systems. He's used to thinking several steps ahead, to anticipating moves and things going wrong and countering them. He is a chess player, and he has played a fantastic game today. He almost had me fooled. But the brother, or whoever he is, wasn't as prepared as he was. He didn't remember the color of Ruby Montgomery's gown, that she didn't have any hair, what arm the IV was in. Don't you think you'd remember those things if you just killed someone for the first time? Wouldn't those things always be with you?

"This is a game for Ted Montgomery. Another complex system for him to manipulate. He killed his wife because she was a burden. Don't you think if she wanted to die, she would've tried to protect her husband? Maybe left a will or some sort of document stating that's what she wanted? She didn't, because she didn't want it. Ted took her life into his own hands and ended it. And this game is the result."

She leaned in close to the jurors, looking them all in the eyes.

"Don't be fooled by this master chess player. See through it. He killed Ruby Montgomery, because Ruby's life was inconvenient for him. And the worst part is that he dragged his children into it, so it all seemed more authentic. His children will never recover from watching their mother die. Never. He destroyed his entire family because it was the convenient thing to do. Do not let him get away with that. Please. Convict him as the murderer that he is."

Debra sat back down. Her jaw muscles flexed and then relaxed before she turned to Brigham. They held each other's gaze until he stood up and crossed the well. He stood in front of the jury with his hands down by his sides. For a long while, he didn't say anything. The silence in the courtroom seemed to echo in his ears, judging him. Calling him a blind fool. Mocking him.

"When I was a kid," he said, "my grandfather on my father's side was a convicted felon who wanted nothing to do with me. But my grandfather on my mother's side was my life. He took me fishing, he taught me about girls, how to drive. He gave me my first drink of beer while we watched a football game. My dad ran off, and he's all I had." Brigham smiled and looked away to the witness stand. "But he smoked. A lot. Sometimes as much as four packs a day. He said it was a gift from World War II. There'd been times in the Pacific jungles where he couldn't do anything but smoke.

"When I turned twelve, two days after my birthday, he told me and my mom about the cancer. Lung cancer. For about three months, it didn't change anything. He would just cough more than usual. At the three-month mark, he began coughing up blood. At nine months, he had to be hospitalized." Brigham looked at the jury and, as much as he fought them, felt the tears running down his cheeks. "I remember coming to his hospital bed." Brigham stared off into the distance, almost seeing the bed. "I would come to his hospital bed, and he'd cry from the pain. They didn't have medications like they do now. They gave him what they could, but it barely touched it. And my grandfather, the toughest man I ever knew, would cry to me that he wished someone would end his pain."

Brigham took a few steps back and leaned against the witness box. "I wished I had the strength to do it, to end his suffering. But I never did. I had to watch him fight for months, in an agony I couldn't even imagine." He swallowed. "And then one day, we got a call from the hospice that he wasn't doing well. We needed to come see him because he was asking for us. We went down there. He'd been a huge guy, six-two and over two hundred pounds. But when I saw him last, he looked like a skeleton. A breeze could knock him out of bed. He was delirious with pain and meds and wasn't making sense, didn't understand that we were there to say goodbye. My mother and I waited around in his room for a long time. But my grandfather started screaming. They sedated him, or tried to, but he wouldn't stop, and they asked us to wait in the lobby. Within two hours, my grandfather was dead.

"There was nothing peaceful about my grandfather's death. It was filled with nothing but pain and terror. And I wish, every day I wish, that I had had the strength to save him all those months of pain. To give him a proper goodbye and a little bit of peace before he left this earth. But I was too weak. I couldn't do it." Brigham looked at Tim and pointed to him. "I wish I'd had a brother like Tim who could've done what I couldn't do. The right thing."

He paused a long time and then walked back in front of the jury. "There's no game here. No chess player. Just a man who had a terrible choice to make, and his brother, believing it to be the right thing, did it for him. Tim told you he will probably be charged with the death of Ruby Montgomery by taking the stand, but he did it anyway." Brigham looked each juror in the eyes. "You swore an oath that you would uphold the law. Well, the law says you can only convict my client if there is proof beyond a reasonable doubt, the highest standard of proof in the law. You have to be almost certain, almost *certain*, that my client committed this crime to convict him. How can we be certain when another man, at the risk of being put on trial himself, is saying he committed the crime?

"My client isn't a mastermind. My client is a grieving husband who doesn't know how he's going to raise three kids on his own. Timothy Montgomery ended Ruby's suffering. But Ted's is just beginning. Please don't add to it."

Brigham stood silent a moment, and then sat down. Debra gave a quick rebuttal, outlining all the inconsistencies in Tim's testimony, and then sat back down.

The judge said, "Ladies and gentlemen of the jury, you will now retire to the jury room for deliberation. If any of you need to use the restrooms beforehand, my bailiff will escort you."

Everyone rose as the jury filed out. Everyone except

Brigham, who was still staring off at nothing, unable to move.

39

When the judge asked if there was anything else while the jury deliberated, Debra said no, but Brigham didn't. He just rose and shook his head. He felt as though he were moving through a swamp with ankle weights. Every action, even every thought, felt as if it would crush him and take all of his energy.

"Okay, folks," Judge Lawrence said, "we're in recess for deliberation."

Brigham didn't wait for anyone to speak to him. He began hurrying out of the courtroom and noticed Molly in the back of the audience, behind some reporters. She smiled at him, but he just looked down and charged out the double doors and into the hall. Behind him, he heard Ted say something, but he didn't respond. He felt hot, and it was difficult to breathe.

Brigham got outside. The sky was overcast with gray clouds, but it wasn't raining. Across the street was the City and County Building, and they had massive lawns with benches on every side. He crossed the street and sat down. Leaning his head back, he stared at the sky and hoped for rain, for some sensation on his skin, because right now he felt numb.

"You didn't wait for me," Molly said, sitting next to him.

"Sorry. I'm not feeling myself right now. It feels like everything is black."

She put her hand on his thigh. "Are you okay?"

"No, I'm definitely not okay."

A long silence between them followed, and Molly kept her hand on him.

"That stuff about your grandfather. Why didn't you ever tell me?"

"I don't like thinking about it." He leaned forward. "You know, the worst part for me, more than seeing him in that type of pain, was that I didn't get to say goodbye. How selfish is that? This man raised me as his son, and when he died screaming in pain, the only thing I can think of is that I didn't get to say goodbye to him in that final moment and hold his hand."

"You're human, Brigham. Just like everybody else. Tommy always used to say that they call your gut your second brain, but it should be your first. You don't have to apologize for feeling the way you do. You were a kid who missed his grandpa."

He leaned on her shoulder. "I…"

"What?"

"There's something horrible I know… and I can't tell anyone."

"Then don't. We'll just sit here and hold each other."

They held each other that way for a long time. Brigham

felt himself drifting. She felt so good, just her touch, her smell, and the way she held him. He wished he could be with her forever, to never let her go. Right now, Brigham wanted nothing to do with trials or courts, or clients. He wanted to be in her arms and nothing else.

Brigham's cell phone buzzed. It was the court.

"This is Brigham," he said.

The court clerk said, "Counselor, we have a verdict."

"That fast?"

"Yup. Eight minutes. New record for us on a homicide."

"I'll be up."

He slipped the phone into his pocket and looked at Molly, her soft eyes, and the way they held him: no judgment, no vindictiveness.

He looked away, out to the cars on the street, and said, "I love you."

She placed her hand in his. "I love you, too."

Brigham rose and marched back to the courthouse, never letting go of her hand.

Ted was out in front of the courtroom with his children. He saw Brigham walking toward them and said, "Before we go in, can I talk to you?"

Brigham opened the door to an Attorney/Client room and

held it for Ted. He stepped inside, and Brigham shut the door and sat across from him at the circular table. Ted crossed his legs, interlacing his fingers on his knee. Brigham held his gaze.

"I'm sorry about your grandfather."

Brigham was quiet a moment. "Yeah."

"Crazy what one cancer cell can lead to."

Brigham nodded, not moving his eyes from Ted's and not responding. Ted grinned at him, and the two men were silent until Ted said, "You know, don't you?"

Brigham waited a beat before answering. "Yes."

"When did you figure it out?"

"When Tim said the IV was in the left arm. It's in the right arm on all the videos. On the left side of the bed were two side tables, with flowers on them from you and the kids. He couldn't have been wrong about that... unless he never saw her in the hospital."

"Then why'd you fight so hard?"

"My job is to fight for you, guilty or innocent."

Ted made a clicking sound through his teeth. "Yeah, that was a great question about the IV. That prosecutor was sharp. I mean, she was wrong about why, but she was sharp. Tim's never been the sharpest tack in the pack, but he's the only brother I have."

"They might come after him. But I'm guessing you'll be testifying at his trial that it was you."

He smiled. "Three million split two ways can buy a lot of loyalty."

"Why lie about it? If you wanted her dead, you could've gone to Oregon."

He shook his head. "Euthanasia negates the life insurance policy. So does murder. But if there's no murder *conviction*, policy pays out."

"Yeah, but the policy was taken out seven years… seven years ago." Brigham's heart dropped into his stomach. "You've been planning this for seven years?" he said quietly.

"Seven nothing. I was going to wait until the kids were older. Teenagers. The cancer was just a happy coincidence. When I did it, you know, she just had this look of shock on her face. Like how could I do something like that to her. Odd how you can share your life with someone for twenty years and still not really know who they are at all. But at least she got to say bye to the kids. She kept it together for them and didn't mention it."

"You could've divorced her."

"Divorce doesn't give me a three-million-dollar life insurance policy tax free, now, does it? The marriage was over, it was just a matter of what I could get out of it."

"You brought your kids to watch her die."

"They had to say bye to their mother. I figured it'd be good closure for them. Then they could focus on whoever I marry next. Truly accept her as their new mom."

Brigham shook his head, not believing what he was hearing. "You waited almost a decade, knowing you were going to kill her. You slept with her, ate meals with her, celebrated birthdays and anniversaries, and you knew you were going to kill her? What kind of monster are you?"

He rose, and adjusted his tie, before winking. "A rich one. Oh, and I know you can't reveal anything we just discussed, but if you do, I will have your Bar license, and we both know it can't be used in court against me, anyway. So this'll just be our little thing."

"Why did you choose me?"

He shrugged. "You were just inexperienced enough to believe me."

Brigham felt empty and cold, as if he were watching this from the outside. But there was nothing he could do but go back into the courtroom and hope that the jury saw Ted for what he was.

Brigham followed Ted and Rebecca into the courtroom, Molly behind him. Scotty was there, too, sitting in the audience. He mouthed the words "good luck" as Brigham walked back, and Brigham had to quickly look away.

He sat at the defense table as the judge came out and the jury shortly after. Ted was next to him, his hands on the table.

"Would the foreman please rise," the judge said.

A large man in a gray sport coat stood up.

"It is my understanding that the jury has reached a verdict," Judge Lawrence said.

"We have, Your Honor," the man said.

"Please pass it to my bailiff."

The bailiff took the verdict form and gave it to the judge. The judge read it passively and then handed it back to the bailiff.

"And what say you in this matter?" the judge asked.

"Your Honor, we find the defendant, Ted Montgomery, not guilty on the sole count of homicide in the first degree."

Sounds of elation and relief came from the audience. Monica began to cry. Several reporters talked among themselves, and Scotty shouted something like, "Woo hoo."

The judge ignored it and said, "Ladies and gentlemen of the jury, I would like to thank you for your time. If you would like to remain after, sometimes the attorneys like to speak with you about the verdict. It's optional, and you are free to leave now if you wish."

Brigham stood up and hurried out of the courtroom without talking to anybody.

40

Brigham was on the roof of his office building. Night had fallen and the stars were out. The grayness of the day had faded away and there was nothing but a clear blackness around him. He pulled a note out from his pocket and read it again.

Dear Brigham, thank you for everything you did. I couldn't have done it without you. Sincerely, T. Montgomery.

He ripped the note into pieces.

He had figured out that Ted was lying to him during Tim's testimony but had thought he had no choice but to continue and fight as hard as he could. He was Ted's lawyer, and clients lied to him all the time anyway. But he thought Ted was lying to get off and to protect Tim at the same time; that he really *had* wanted to give her peace but also wanted to be around for his kids. Brigham couldn't have even guessed that money was the motivation for killing his wife. The real question was if Brigham had known that, would he still have continued with the trial?

Molly stepped out the door on the roof leading down to the offices and came over to him. She leaned against the edge and looked down.

"I figured you'd be up here again," she said. "You should

be out celebrating. Ted offered to take everyone at the firm out for the fanciest dinner we've ever had."

"I'm not very hungry."

She wrapped her arm around his. "You did a great job. You should be proud."

"He did it, Molly. I can't tell you why, but he did it."

She nodded. "I knew that from the moment he got up on that stand. It doesn't matter. It's not your job to worry about that."

"Isn't it? This guy... I've never met anyone like him. He's not human."

She rested her head on his shoulder. "But you are. You have a kind heart, and you believed him. It's not your fault. Even if he would've told you everything you know now when he signed up, would you have defended him just as hard?"

"Maybe..." She looked at him. "Yes," he finally said, "yes, I would've defended him just as hard."

"Then it doesn't matter. You did your job."

"He told me I was just inexperienced enough to believe him."

"It's not inexperience. You have a good heart. That's not a bad thing." She looked him in the eyes. "Let's go out and eat. Just me and you."

He nodded. "Just me and you."

"Yup."

He kissed her, and she led him off the roof.

The next morning, Brigham had court for Jessica Padilla in the Salt Lake City Justice Court. He was still in a foggy haze, and riding his bike to the court felt like a high-wire act in which he could fall over and break his neck at any moment.

Jen, his investigator, had found out why the chief prosecutor wasn't giving deals on Jessica Padilla. It turned out that Jessica Padilla's husband had gone to college with the chief prosecutor and they had been quite the item but broke up somewhere around junior year. Jessica had been blamed as the new love of his life. Brigham would use that information to get the chief prosecutor to back down. The last thing she probably wanted was her love life discussed in court or among defense attorneys.

He got to the court and an older bailiff saw him. He set his satchel down and prepared to go through the metal detectors and then get wanded. The bailiff smiled at him and waved him through.

"I recognize you, Counselor. Go ahead."

Brigham slipped through without getting wanded. As he took the stairs heading up to his courtroom, despite the fatigue and haziness, a smile crept onto his lips.

CPSIA information can be obtained
at www.ICGtesting.com
Printed in the USA
LVHW111455260819
628954LV00001B/363/P